WE BOTH CAN'T BE BAE 3

WRITTEN BY:
TWYLA T

PUBLISHER'S NOTE

This is a work of fiction. Names, characters, places, and events are strictly the product of the author or used fictitiously. Any similarities between actual persons, living or dead, events, settings, or locations are entirely coincidental.

Text **COLEHART** to 22828 to sign up for the mailing list and updates on new releases.

DEDICATION

This series is dedicated in memory of my baby brother, Hassan Turner. I have been reading since I was a teenager, and in the back of my mind I always said I should write a book one day. I never found or made time to write until after I lost my baby brother at the tender age of 23 in a tragic drowning accident July 19, 2015. To make matters worse, my mom had a massive stroke the day before my brother's funeral. I didn't know how to go on, but I knew I had to because so many people depend on me. My closest family and friends encouraged me every day to find an outlet and it was then that I finally MADE time to write. I sat down on November 6, 2015, and I have been writing daily since then. Writing has become therapeutic for me and has kept me sane. It is my hope that you enjoy the ride in this series, which I have created for you during my therapy. Keep resting baby brother. I love and miss you dearly!!

ACKNOWLEDGEMENTS

Writing this book has been a dream come true to me. It has been an exciting and satisfying journey all because of God and my awesome support system. I feel so grateful to be able to finally do what I absolutely love. I have far too many people who have encouraged and inspired me to name one by one, but each and every one of you know how much I love and appreciate you. It's more than words can even describe. I hope that each of you enjoy this series as much as I enjoyed writing it. Thanks so much for taking a chance on me. Enjoy and be blessed!!

WE BOTH CAN'T BE BAE 3
BY:
AUTHOR TWYLA T.

If you haven't read parts 1 & 2, go catch up now before turning the page!!!!

As always, I want your honest feedback. Please leave me a review on Amazon and/ or any of my social media sites and I promise I will read them all. You may also reach me via email at authortwylat@gmail.com . My Facebook, Instagram, and Twitter handles are @authortwylat.

Prologue

"I'm pregnant," Phebe blurted out to Luke as they were driving down the highway heading home. They had spent yesterday and last night together, while Keith was out of town handling business. He did a double take and almost lost control of the car. Once it registered what she said, he started grinning like a kid on Christmas morning.

"Word, well, I know for a fact now that it's time for me to make you all mine," Luke said. She smiled, relieved that he was happy. "So, how far along are you?" he asked. She told him that she was only a couple of months. The next thing she told him was about how Keith knew her cycle and ovulating days like clockwork, how she faked her cycle, and slept with him on a day when she should have been ovulating, knowing she was already pregnant. Luke was a bit angered by her actions, but he told her that he understood and he didn't want any more games. Phebe had no idea that she had dialed Keith's cell and a voicemail was being left on his phone.

Out of nowhere, gunshots rang out like fireworks on the fourth of July. POW POW POW POW POW POW POW!!! Blood splattered everywhere and screams could be heard before Luke lost control of the car and swerved off of the road, flipping a couple of times and finally landing in a ditch. The car behind them timed everything perfectly and exited the highway like nothing had happened, heading to ditch the stolen car, retrieve theirs, and inform their boss that the job had been taken care of.

RECAP

Malcolm eased out before any of the women could look his way. While they were all in shock about the secret that was revealed before them, he took that opportunity to escape in peace. There was no telling what else might transpire at Charlotte's house, but he was not about to stick around to see. The graze from the gunshot wound on his arm was stinging and burning like hell, but going to the hospital was out of the question. Malcolm knew he would have to give a story about what happened and that would involve talking to the cops, and he hated police. The officers who wanted him arrested for Cameron's accident had finally stopped harassing him. It took Malcolm paying them five stacks each to back off, but he wasn't sure it was completely over. They didn't know that he pulled in that amount in one week and it was really chump change to him.

As Malcolm was driving away, he started thinking back to how all of this started. He tried to stop sneaking around with Charlotte several times, but she would never take no for an answer. In fact, on this very trip, he was only stopping by to end things once and for all, but when she broke down crying about how her whole life was a lie, he couldn't bring himself to do so. Malcolm initially had Charlotte believing that Cameron hated her guts and bad-mouthed her often. Charlotte was obsessed with Cameron's life and it didn't take much to convince her to give up the pussy; she really threw it to Malcolm before he ever asked. Malcolm thought about how it all began…

Before Mr. Miller finally got Cameron to agree to marry me, we had several conversations. He almost backed out more times than one, but he really didn't want me to tell what I knew about him. I felt like blackmailing him; to get such a beautiful woman was well worth it. His oldest daughter, Charlotte, was pretty, but I didn't care for light-skinned women. I wanted his beautiful chocolate daughter and I had him right where I wanted him after I found out some information about him at work. In the deal we made, I agreed to leave the job and start driving trucks cross country, which is the job I had just started, due to a great referral, when I met Cameron.

On the night of the rehearsal dinner, Charlotte overheard us saying something about the "arrangement" and she approached me afterwards. I didn't know how much she heard, so I wasn't about to give anything away. "So, what are you willing to do to keep me from telling my sister about this arrangement between you and our dad?" Charlotte asked me.

"What are you talking about?" I asked her, trying to play dumb.

"Don't try to play me, Malcolm. I heard y'all," she replied.

"Well, you tell me what you heard and I'll tell you what I will do to keep you from telling her," I said to her. I had her right there because she couldn't say anything. Well, I thought I had her. She walked away and we went into the sanctuary of the church for rehearsal. Charlotte was eyeing me the entire time. I tried to ignore her, but it was very hard. I started thinking that maybe I should have given her a chance, instead of Cameron. We made it through the rehearsal and rehearsal dinner with ease. As soon as the dinner was over, Cameron bolted out of the door. I knew she was excited to get to her bachelorette party, so I sent her a text telling her to have fun because she would only have one bachelorette party in life. I didn't want a bachelor party the night before my wedding because I knew how out of hand it would get, which is why I had one the weekend before and it was one for the books.

Cameron never texted back and I assumed she was with her girls having a good time. They said they wouldn't have strippers and I hoped they weren't lying, but I couldn't be so sure, which is why I was planning to pop up on them. My plans were changed when I was trying to walk out of the bathroom at the church and Charlotte walked in, pushing me backwards. "So, do I have to tell my sister about this arrangement or do you want to know more about the black car she just jumped in and left?" Charlotte said to me. I stood there speechless. Charlotte never gave me a chance to answer before she kissed me passionately and grabbed my dick. The way she massaged brought it to attention immediately. "If you won't tell, neither will I. This won't even count as cheating since you aren't married yet," Charlotte whispered in my ear.

I thought about what she said. I knew it was wrong, but with the way she had been staring at me all night, I was very turned on. I picked Charlotte up, placed her on the counter, and tongued her down. She unbuckled my pants and pulled her shirt over her head. "Just this one time," I told her. She agreed and I dove into her pussy. She dug her nails into my back as I pumped for dear life. After a couple of minutes, I pulled out and my nut landed on her thighs.

"Wait, you mean to tell me you a two-minute brother with this decent sized dick? You gonna have to come with me. We changing our agreement to one night, instead of one time," Charlotte said. Her comment kinda insulted my manhood, but since she offered, I went to her hotel room that night. What was supposed to be a one-night fling turned into us sneaking around behind Cameron's back our entire marriage. Getting caught never really crossed my mind because the two of them never got along and I sure as hell didn't expect them to make a surprise visit. I don't know how the hell I'm gonna get out of this shit.

Charlotte knew she was wrong, but she felt like the lies that had been kept from her justified her actions. As she was sitting there on the floor, she thought back to how she got into this mess.

The night before my sister's wedding, I was upset because my dad was jumping head over heels to make sure his baby girl's wedding day was perfect. I know it wasn't their fault that I jumped up and got married without telling them, but everything was always about Cameron. EVERYTHING!! It didn't help that my marriage didn't even last a full year and, here, my baby sister was about to marry a man who was already pulling in six figures. When I saw my dad and Malcolm talking in the corner, they were looking guilty, so I decided to sneak up and try to hear what they were whispering about. By the time I made it close to them, the conversation was ending, but I could tell that my dad was upset and I heard him say something about wishing he had never made this arrangement with Malcolm. I decided to play on that and act like I knew what was up. I should have never approached Malcolm. After that two minutes in the bathroom at the church, I should have really been done, but I felt like I was in control and wanted more. After we left the church and went to my hotel room, Malcolm made up for his two-minute game with that tongue of his. He had me climbing the walls. He wouldn't let me go down on him that night and I was a bit hurt because I wanted to return the favor. A year later, he opened up to me about his childhood and I understood why he never wanted head, and I told him I wouldn't pressure him. He said it was easy to talk to me. He told me that Cameron hated me and talked about me all the time, so I saw no reason to stop fucking him. I did feel guilty at times, but Malcolm always told me something that Cameron said or did every time I tried to break things off.

A few weeks ago, when I made it home, a car was parked in my driveway. I was irritated because everyone I dealt with knew not to park in my driveway, so I had no idea who was parked there. When I pulled up behind the car and got out, a woman who looked a lot like my mom got out. "Hi Charlotte, I know you don't know me and I have a lot of explaining to do, but I'm your mom," is what the lady said. I looked at her like the lunatic she was and told her, if she didn't leave my home within the next minute, I was calling the cops. I guess she didn't take me very serious because she kept standing there trying to talk until I pulled my cellphone and mace from my purse. "I know this is a bit strange, but please hear me out," she said.

"You have less than thirty seconds left to leave my house," I said, as I walked right past her and into the house. When I made it inside, I looked out the window and she was sitting in her car. She sat there for about two more minutes before finally backing out.

After the woman left, I told myself that it was time to finally get an alarm system, and a gun wouldn't be a bad idea because if someone is bold enough to show up at your house saying they are your mom, then there is no telling what else they might do.

Later on that night, I jumped when my doorbell rang, completely forgetting that Malcolm was stopping by. That lady who said she was my mom had me shook. I had been thinking about her for the past few hours, wondering why she resembled my mom so much. "A lady came by here today and said she was my mom," I told Malcolm.

"What? What are you talking about?" he asked me. I told him how everything happened and he sat there like he was in deep thought. I couldn't figure out what he was thinking, but I knew that he knew something by the change in his body language. At that moment, I had no idea about the exact details of the "arrangement" my dad and Malcolm had made, but as he talked, the pieces started falling into place. I slapped the shit of him because I realized right then that he had played me and my entire family.

I sat there in a daze, thoughts running wild. I thought Malcolm would leave after I slapped him, but he knew he had fucked up. I really didn't know whose life was more fucked up, mine or his. He leaned over and started massaging my breasts through my tank top. Sex with Malcolm had gotten better as time passed by. We both had agreed not to get our feelings caught up in each other because we knew what we were doing was already wrong. I knew he had a couple of other women he was sleeping with anyway. I got wet from his touch, but sex wasn't on my mind at the time. I had some shit I needed to figure out. I told him that he could stay, but I needed some time to process everything that was happening.

The next morning when I got up and got ready for work, I was still confused. My mom, or who I thought was my mom, had called and left a voicemail and she had even texted me. I didn't want to be bothered with anyone and I definitely didn't want to confront her and be dead wrong about everything. I decided to keep my distance for a while, which wasn't out of the norm for me anyway. When I walked out to get in my car, there was an envelope on the windshield with the words, **PLEASE READ!!** I pretty much knew it had to be a letter from the mystery woman that stopped by yesterday. I grabbed it and put it in my purse and told myself that I would read it on my lunch break. I hated my job and really wanted to call in, but I had bills to pay.

I took a few calls and after a lady cussed me out about something she ordered but didn't want to pay for, I put my phone on hold to look like I was still on a call and pulled the envelope from my purse. When I opened it, four pictures fell out. One was a baby picture of me, one was a picture of me and the woman who said she was my mom, one was a picture of my parents, and the last one was a picture of my two moms, I guess. I was scared to open the letter after examining the pictures for about five minutes straight. I finally gathered up enough nerves to open it.

I can't even imagine the thoughts that are running through your mind, but the first thing I need to say is; I'M SO SORRY!!! I really am your real mother and the woman that raised you is my sister. I made some terrible mistakes in the past, and the biggest one was leaving you. I was upset that things didn't turn out the way I felt like they should. I did a terrible thing to my sister and my life has never been the same since then. Words can't even describe how sorry I am. I know you must feel like your life is a lie, but that's not true. Charles is your father and Carla has been the best mother possible. I know it was hard on her, but she treated you like you were her very own. She never wanted anything else to do with me and I can't blame her. Every letter I sent was always returned without even being opened. I went to have an abortion after I found out I was pregnant with you, but I just couldn't go through with it. I know you must be wondering why I am bringing all of this up now. That's a fair question, but it is also difficult. I would rather not get into all of that on this letter. I would love to meet you for dinner, so we can talk face to face. I plan on meeting with your parents within the next month, but don't mention anything about me until we talk please. Meet me at the Bistro on Main Street tonight at 7:30 please. Just ask for Crystal if you decide to come. I pray that you will.

After reading that letter, I couldn't do anymore work. I barely did anything before, but I certainly couldn't function after, so I left work for the day and went home. I wanted to stop

14

by the liquor store, but my brain couldn't register anything except to go straight home, and that's what I did. I went home and got straight in the bed and cried. I cried about all of the things that I had done in life. I cried wondering what my life would have been like if my real mom would have raised me, instead of my aunt. I cried trying to figure out if Cameron and I would have been closer if we would have been raised as the first cousins we were, instead of sisters. I always thought my mom treated me and Cameron different, but now I wondered if it was just me all along not feeling the connection that they seemed to have. I had too many unanswered questions. I must have finally drifted off to sleep because the sun was setting when I woke up. My eyes were red and puffy and I had a headache. I grabbed a pen and a piece of paper and wrote a note.

Crystal,

I am really not sure what to say to you and I just can't face you right now. My whole life has been turned upside down because of you. How do you give me away and disappear for twenty-three years? My mom loves me, but I never felt a connection to her and it's all because of you. So, you and dad had an affair and you just gave me to them to raise? How have you slept at night all of these years? There is so much that I want to say, but I'm not sure if it's even worth it. Why did you come back now? Give your number to Jimmy that works at the restaurant and I will get it from him. Give me some time to process all of this information and I will get back with you when I have the energy to deal with all of this.

I took that letter and dropped it off at the Bistro because I didn't want to face Crystal. Eventually, I knew that I would have to, but I couldn't that day. A stop by the liquor store was not missed before I headed back home. I knew I was gonna need something to calm my nerves. At that moment, I knew for sure that I had to end things with Malcolm. Cameron was still my sister, despite the circumstances that popped up, and it was time to cut the bullshit, which is why Malcolm was at my house when they popped up. I know what it must have looked like, but he really was just about to hop in the shower. I asked him to open the door because one of my home girls was about to stop by and I assumed it was her. Never in a million years did I think my mom and Cameron would be on the other side of the door. I can't blame Cameron for shooting at us, but I'm glad she didn't kill anyone. Now, here we all are, each person lost in their own thoughts.

Cameron looked at her mom and then she looked at her sister. As she scanned the room, she noticed that Malcolm was nowhere in sight. She got up and picked up her gun that was sitting beside her mom. Neither Mrs. Miller nor Charlotte budged, which confirmed that everyone was in shock. The house was eerily quiet. Cameron had never been in her sister's home before, but that didn't stop her from going from room to room looking for Malcolm. He was nowhere to be found. Cameron went and opened the front door and noticed that his truck was gone. "That black motherfucker left!" Cameron said to herself.

Cameron started thinking about how fucked up her life was. Blowing Charlotte's brains out crossed her mind, but she couldn't bring herself to shoot her in front of their mom. Malcolm was the one who had caused all of this drama and bullshit and was the one who needed to pay. *If I would have just been a woman and did what I wanted to do, none of this would have happened. Why didn't I just leave him? He's killing me slowly anyway. Malcolm is gonna pay for all of this. There is no other way around it,* Cameron thought to herself. She bent down and picked her purse up from the floor that she dropped on the way in and retrieved her cellphone to call him. Malcolm answered the phone, but no words ever left his mouth. Cameron was too furious to speak, so the line was just silent. Tears streamed down her face. After two whole minutes of silence, Cameron held the gun upward and fired it.

On the other end of the phone, Malcolm was speechless. He knew that Cameron would be calling soon and there was no sense in ignoring her because he had truly fucked up. She was silent, which meant she was fed up, because her mouth was too smart and slick to be quiet. Malcolm knew it was best to remain quiet until she spoke. He heard sniffling and then her voice was low, but he heard her say, "You have fucked over me for the last time and I refuse to live like this anymore," and then a gunshot rang out loud!

Malcolm almost lost control of his truck. He had made it about twenty miles away from Charlotte's house, but he knew he had to get back there as quick as possible. He cried and cried and had to pull over. He called Cameron's phone about twenty times, but she never answered. Malcolm called Charlotte's phone next, but she didn't pick up either. Traffic was heavy and it would take him longer to get back, but he was headed back to see just what had happened.

Back In Mississippi

Kingston ran into his Paw Paw's arms as soon as he spotted him after school. He was so happy because he knew he was about to have the best weekend ever. Right after leaving the school, Kingston asked were they gonna go fishing. "Of course we are," his granddad answered. Fishing was one of Mr. Miller's favorite things to do and he had taken Kingston a few times, and he loved it. They headed out to Choctaw Lake, so they could get a couple of hours in before dark. When they made it, Mr. Miller put a life jacket on Kingston, then himself, before loading and getting into the speed boat.

Within the first three minutes, Mr. Miller got a bite on his line, so he switched rods with Kingston to let him reel in it. Kingston was super excited that he caught the first fish. They stayed out there about an hour and a half and caught a total of four fish. Two of them were too small to keep, so Kingston threw them back. Mr. Miller already knew where Kingston wanted to go next, so he went ahead and headed towards McDonald's without him having to ask. When they made it, Kingston ran straight to the play land. After he played for about twenty minutes, they went inside to order. "May I have a cheeseburger kid's meal-" Mr. Miller started, but was cut off.

"I want a man's meal like you, Paw Paw. Get me a quarter pounder with fries and a Coke," Kingston said.

"Well, just give us two quarter pounder meals with Cokes, please ma'am," Mr. Miller said to the cashier while laughing.

"Hey granny!" Kingston said as he took off running to hug a lady that walked up behind them.

"Granny?" Mr. Miller asked.

"Yes Paw Paw, she told me I can call her granny," Kingston said.

Mr. Miller didn't know what to say, so he just introduced himself.

"I know who you are. I'm Mrs. Edwards."

The ticket number to their food was called, so Mr. Miller told her it was nice to meet her. He didn't want to question Kingston about why he was calling this strange woman granny, but he was sure going to ask his daughter.

Later that night while Mr. Miller was in the back, the doorbell rang. Ding dong...ding dong...ding dong!! Mr. Miller couldn't get to the door fast enough. Whoever was on the other end was being very impatient. "I'll get it Paw Paw," Kingston said while running towards the front door, almost knocking his granddad over.

"Wait a second son..." Mr. Miller tried to say, but Kingston had already opened the door.

"Well, hello, little fella; aren't you just as cute as can be!" said the voice at the door. Charles froze dead in his tracks, not believing he was hearing this voice he hadn't heard in a few years.

"What in the world are you doing here?" Mr. Miller asked.

Chapter 1

"Well, it's good to see you too, Charles," Crystal said. "And look at this little cutie right here. You must be Kingston," she continued. Kingston stood there looking back and forth between the two adults, wanting to say something, but not knowing exactly what to say, so he remained quiet and just stared at both of them.

He finally broke his silence by saying "You look a little like my granny number one!"

They both looked at him while having their own separate thoughts, but elected to just ignore him. "What are you doing here, Crystal?" Mr. Miller asked again nervously. Sweat beams had started to form on his head, and he wiped them off and rubbed his hands on his pants. He thought that when she appeared a few years ago, that would be the last that he would have to see of her. It cost him so much and he was still paying for it. Cameron had suffered the most because of him and his inconsiderate decisions. She was the ultimate sacrifice and had no idea just what her dad had done for his own selfish reasons. Mr. Miller started thinking back to how all of the madness began…

The new custodial worker always seemed weird, but he was always nice, so I made it my business to talk to him and keep him near. It seemed that he needed some extra support, so I kinda took him in. I could tell that he was a bit shaky around the edges. Malcolm was his name. I invited him to a baseball game that I had extra tickets to one weekend and that sealed the deal with the relationship that we had started to build. I don't think he had ever gone to a game before and since my son, Fred, was in the army, I didn't mind taking him. Talking to me every day became a mission of his after that. He would always ask about my baby girl, Cameron, after I caught him staring at a family picture that was on my desk. He asked to meet her, but I didn't think it was a good idea. It really didn't feel right. I was starting to look at him as a son, but not necessarily a son-in-law. He asked me about taking her out several times, but I always told him no. He never stopped asking, even with me knowing that he flirted with and talked to other women.

"You can't expect for me to hand you over to my daughter with me knowing how freely you flirt with women," I said to him.

"I won't be this way when I settle down. I promise," Malcolm replied. I tried to tell him that he must start making changes before even thinking about settling down, but he blew me off with the wave of his hand and kept right on talking about taking Cameron out on a date.

A few months later, Malcolm had just left out of my office and only about two minutes passed before there was a knock on my door. Thinking that it was my receptionist bringing me the monthly report, I said come in without even looking up. After thirty or so seconds passed, I heard someone clear their throat. While still looking down, I told her thanks and to place the report on my desk. I was very busy trying to seal a deal I had been working on for the past few months. Working as the senior project manager for one of the top construction companies in the states had its perks, but it could also be overwhelming at times. I made it my business to try to stay ten steps ahead of the competition. Malcolm would eventually work at one of the sites, but he had to start out at the bottom just like everyone else did with the company is what I started thinking when I saw his file and thought about him asking to be promoted already. When she didn't drop the folder on the desk, I finally looked up. Looking at Crystal, I thought I saw a ghost. To say that I was shocked would be an understatement. I hadn't laid eyes on that woman since she dropped Charlotte off with us over twenty years ago.

"Long time no see huh," Crystal said. I was speechless. Anger that I had for her started to resurface because of how she had handled things. I didn't regret raising Charlotte at all, but a better plan could have been put into play. At times, I still can't believe my marriage withstood that test, but it sure as hell wasn't easy. I can't count the counseling sessions we attended together and individually. Sometimes, I still think that Carla holds a small grudge and if she ever stepped out on me, I wouldn't have any

other choice but to deal with it. We made it through, but to look up into Crystal's eyes had me seeing red.

"What the hell are you doing here?" I asked through gritted teeth.

"Please calm down Charles. I know that work would be the only place that I could catch you by yourself, so I decided to go for it after all the contemplating I've been doing," Crystal said.

"Why are you here?" I asked again.

I just need to talk to you. I can't tell you how sorry I am for what I did. I want to make things right," she said.

"Make things right! Make things right! Just what in the hell does that mean; how can you make things right?" I asked while becoming angrier.

"I want my daughter back," Crystal said. I hopped up out of my chair so fast that the chair hit the wall and made a loud boom. I walked around the desk and temporarily thought about choking the shit out of her, but my senses kicked in and I calmed down. I had never laid hands on a woman and wasn't about to start. She must have saw my mood change because within seconds, she started crying and she threw her arms around me. I started to feel bad for her, so I lifted my arms that had been hanging stubbornly by my sides and gave her a hug to try to comfort her. I briefly had thoughts of the few moments that we shared, and she must have felt it in my body language because she leaned up and kissed me. It was a sweet, soft, and sensual kiss.

I pulled back after about five seconds that seemed like an eternity after I heard a male voice clear his throat. It was Malcolm. I noticed his phone in his hand, but I had no idea that he had taken pictures of me hugging Crystal, and even the kiss, until the next day when he demanded that I get him a date with Cameron.

I didn't take heed to his threat initially, but when I noticed that he had photo shopped several pictures of Crystal and myself, I had to give in. He had pictures of us naked while

21

hugging and kissing. I had a baby with this woman, my wife's sister, so I knew there was no way she would believe that those pictures were photo shopped because she knew exactly how my office looked. I was caught between a rock and a hard place. In my mind, I figured that Malcolm getting with Cameron wouldn't be such a bad idea. I wanted the best for all of my kids, so I put my plan into action. I knew I wouldn't be able to stand looking at Malcolm on the regular, so I called in a favor to one of my buddies and got him a job driving trucks. Because of my connections, he started out making close to six figures and within six months to a year, he would be making that amount.

After Crystal popped up on that day, it seemed that things took a turn for the worse, so seeing her at this very moment, I was not looking forward to the future.

Chapter 2

Cameron ended the call with Malcolm after she fired her gun into the air. Plaster and dry wall started falling from the ceiling, leaving a small hole from the bullet that had lodged. Within seconds, her mom came running into the living room and Charlotte was right on her heels. "What's going on in here Cameron? What happened?" her mom asked with a panicked expression all over her face.

Cameron didn't even answer; she barely looked up at them. Another call was placed and she immediately started crying and screaming. "HELP! HELP ME PLEASE!! He's going to kill me as soon as he gets back! Please help me. I'm not ready to die. Send someone fast... no, I don't know the address here. I just got here and caught my husband with my sister and he went crazy on me.... ma'am, you don't understand. He is on his way back and he is going to kill me this time. He has tried several times before. He never started back taking his meds and he is crazy! Please help me!" Cameron said to the 911 operator while crying harder. There was silence and she finished up by begging them to please hurry and send help right away because she wasn't ready to die.

"Cameron, sweetheart, what are you doing?" her mom asked.

"Something I should have done a long time ago. I'm sick of him and I never should have let him get away with running me off of the road and almost killing me. I have been stupid long enough. This madness ends today," Cameron said to her mom with finality. Charlotte just stood there, not knowing what to say. She really didn't know all of the details surrounding her sister's 'accident', so she opted to remain silent out of fear of possibly saying the wrong thing. It was clear that she didn't know Malcolm too well. Cameron looked over at Charlotte and pointed the gun at her. "If I really didn't love you, I would blow your mother fuckin' brains out-,"

Cameron started saying, but was interrupted with her mother screaming her name. "CAMERON MILLER! You put that gun down right away," Mrs. Miller said.

"It's Cameron Miller Price, thanks to daddy," Cameron said while still aiming the gun at her sister.

"Just shoot me. Go ahead and shoot me because I don't deserve to live," Charlotte said while tears were rolling down her face. Cameron walked closer and told Charlotte not to tempt her, and their mom stepped between the two of them.

"If you shoot her, you're gonna have to shoot me first. I can't sit here and watch you kill my child," Mrs. Miller said to Cameron.

"You still calling me your child?" Charlotte asked through tears. Crystal has been here and she told me everything," she continued. Charlotte heard Mrs. Miller saying I raised you and I will always be your mother, no matter what, before she started thinking back to the night she finally called Crystal and decided to meet her.

Two weeks had passed since Crystal showed up at my house claiming to be my mom. I wouldn't give her the time of day, so she left a letter on my car and I got it the next morning. She wanted me to meet with her for dinner, but I couldn't bring myself to do so. So, I wrote her a letter back and left it with a guy at the bar. I must have read that letter at least a thousand times in just that short period of time. I probably had it memorized. My emotions were all over the place. I felt everything except happiness because of the things that I had been doing.

I decided to finally meet with Crystal because I felt like she owed me some type of explanation. If you give your child away, there has to be some kinda valid reason, right? Still not knowing whether she was really my mother or not, I went ahead because I couldn't deny the resemblance that she shared with who I knew as my mom my whole life. When I arrived at the restaurant, she got up from the booth to hug me, but I was hesitant. She noticed and said that she understood, but I saw some hurt in her eyes. It was awkward sitting across from her because I didn't know what I was supposed to be feeling.

"I was selfish and there really aren't any words that I can say to make anything right or to make you understand my

actions. If I could do it all over again, I would, but that's impossible. I know that I can't come in and expect for you to just accept me with open arms, but I just need to try to make things right in my life at this point," Crystal said.

"What's going on in your life that made you pop up after all of these years? It can't be just you wanting to make things right because you've had years to try and do that," Charlotte said, not caring anything about Crystal's sad speech.

"I really don't want to go into all of that right now; I just-," she started saying before Charlotte cut her off.

"Listen, you're pretty lucky I'm even sitting here right now. You left me and then popped back up and you're still trying to hide things. I don't have to take this," Charlotte said while standing up and grabbing her purse.

"No, please wait. Just give me a few minutes to explain. It's really difficult," Crystal said, as a single tear slid down her left cheek. She tried to wipe it off before Charlotte noticed, but it was too late. Charlotte sat back down and softened her mood once she saw the true hurt in Crystal's eyes. "I really didn't even want to bring this up because I don't want any sympathy, but I should have known that I wouldn't be able to just pop back up without explaining myself. I have breast cancer. I was diagnosed ten years ago, it went into remission, but now it has returned and it seems to be spreading. I decided not to go through with treatments this time because years ago, the chemotherapy made me feel ten times worse. I didn't want to die without you knowing the truth about things that happened all of those years ago," Crystal said.

"Sit down girls; I have some things that I need to tell y'all. I didn't think I would ever have to have this conversation, but I see now that it is needed," Mrs. Miller said, which caused Charlotte to snap out of her thoughts. Before she could start talking, they heard sirens blasting and Cameron jumped right into her acting mode. Her mother and sister had figured out what she was doing without her even telling them.

Cameron opened the door and took off running and screaming before the police could get to the door. "He's on his way back and he's gonna kill me. He will be here soon. Y'all have to help me!" Cameron said through tears.

"Calm down ma'am! We won't let him hurt you. Tell us exactly what happened," one of the officers said while putting his arm around Cameron, trying to console her.

"I came here with my mother and we were trying to surprise my sister, but we were the ones who got surprised. We caught my husband here with my sister," Cameron said while continuing to sob. The officer glanced at the door at Charlotte and she dropped her head. "He's tried to kill me before, but I wouldn't tell the cops what happened because he told he would finish the job. You can call the police in Mississippi and they will tell you. He's supposed to be taking some kinda medication too, but he's not. I want to have him committed," Cameron said. While she continued her story, the officer to the side was making phone calls.

About three minutes later, Cameron was still crying, but when she heard a vehicle, she looked up and saw Malcolm's truck turning the corner. She took off running and screaming towards the house. The cop had already called for backup and he also made a call to Mississippi to a buddy he knew on the force to verify Cameron's story. When Malcolm got out of the truck, he took off running towards the house. He didn't see Cameron run in, but in his mind, he thought she had shot herself. He never reached the door because the officers drew their weapons on him and he was forced to stop in his tracks. The white officer who made the call was the first to speak up.

"FREEZE AND PUT YOUR HANDS UP!!" he told him. Malcolm looked over to the black cop thinking he would help him out, not knowing anything about the details Cameron had just told them. When they saw a bloody shirt wrapped around his arm, that was enough for them to approach him and handcuff him. Malcolm didn't go down without a fight. He swung on the officers and he connected with the black cop. He was satisfied because in his mind, the brother should have had his back. After jumping down on the cop and choking him for about five long seconds, he was pulled off by the cop's partner. The fight didn't last long, but just enough happened to make them follow through with their plans.

"What did I do? I need to make sure my wife is alright!" Malcolm was pleading with the officers, but all of his words fell on deaf ears. Before the officers made it, Cameron had scratched herself up and she looked like she had been a fight that she was really in. The officers didn't need to know that her fist fight was with her sister; she only needed them to take Malcolm away. When the officer received the call back that he was waiting on, he signaled for his partner to lead Malcolm to the squad car and he walked into the house. Her story about the incident in Mississippi checked out and he was told that they had been waiting on Cameron to come forth. They would never admit to taking money from Malcolm to drop the case. In their minds, he was the fool because they would deny any word he said. One of the officers spoke with Cameron again and let her know that she would have to come down to the police station to make an official statement. She showed him the hole in the ceiling and also the ones in the wall and said that Malcolm had been shooting at her. The cop was so furious with Malcolm that he never asked her how he got his wound. In his eyes, Malcolm was already guilty and if they couldn't hold him on any charges, they were already making arrangements to have him shipped to a mental facility.

After he was finally secure in the car, Malcolm just dropped his head, not knowing what to think. His mind started wandering as he tried to figure out just what the hell was going on. He figured that he would have gone to jail for trying to kill her months back, not for being caught at her sister's house. Flashbacks of everything started to invade his mind and he began to hyperventilate. When he finally looked up and saw Cameron talking to the officers, he became furious. He started banging on the window with his head, then he fell back and started kicking the door with his feet. The more he moved, the tighter the handcuffs got and he yelled out in pain when they started pinching his skin.

"LET ME OUT OF HERE! I DIDN'T DO ANYTHING. I KNOW MY RIGHTS!!" Malcolm continued to yell, not knowing the cops had decided not to take him to jail. They deemed him to be a threat to himself and others, so they called the state hospital. As soon as they arrived on the scene, Malcolm had not calmed down yet, so when they opened the door to the car, they injected him with a dose of Chlorpromazine and he was out within minutes.

Chapter 3

For some strange reason, Cameron was on Keith's mind pretty heavy, but he couldn't call or check on her because Phebe was on him like white on rice. The connection he was feeling to Cameron at that present moment was unreal. It kinda seemed as if she was in some type of trouble. Here lately, Phebe had been asking him about every number he called and texted and even about incoming text messages and calls. He knew that she had a friend who worked at C-Spire and suspected that she had accessed his account because their lines weren't even joined and she knew absolutely too much. *I should call and report her trifling ass,* Keith had thought to himself. She had mentioned him joining the lines and making her the primary number on several different occasions, but he never gave it any serious thought. *I thought you said she was the one always calling you, but it looks like you have been the one making all the calls to that bitch,* he remembered Phebe saying. It was true, he had been calling and texting Cameron since the fight they had. Most times, he would hang up before she could pick up, but she never called back. He wanted to tell Phebe that when you go looking for trouble, you always find the shit, but he just kept it to himself. "Fuck this shit, let me go and meet this new connect real quick," Keith said to himself.

It was late Friday evening and Keith knew he should have left home an hour ago, but his thoughts were all over the place. Getting himself together was a harder task than normal. He was missing out on money and that was unlike him, so he knew he had to snap out of it soon and very soon. His team worked hard, so he was able to relax if he wanted to, but that wasn't his style. He believed in going hard for himself. People would never be able to say he didn't work for everything he had. Niggas were always on the come up, so he knew he had to stay grinding to succeed.

Keith threw on some dark blue Ermenegildo Zegna jeans, a black hoodie, laced up his black Timbs, put on his favorite gold cross chain, grabbed his keys and phone, and he was out. He was headed to meet with a new connect, then he was meeting up at one of his homeboy's house for a little kickback.

Phebe was gonna meet him there later since the crowd was mixed, but he couldn't help but to wish it was Cameron, since she was the one who always went everywhere with him. She was always so laid back and fit right in with everybody. Phebe being at home was very different, but she was adamant on finding a job close to home, so she was there. He had turned down the job that he interviewed for and knew that she would get wind of it and start making a fuss about it soon. She claimed she was so ready for him to go legit, but never acknowledged the fact that his hustle is what paid for all of her schooling, kept her riding in style, up to date with the latest fashions, and kept money in her pockets. Like a regular nine to five would support her habits. Cameron never asked for anything, which was why he always broke her off so freely; Phebe was a whole different story. The streets had been loyal to him so, in his mind, he would always be loyal to the streets.

The business with the connect was A-1 and Keith was now headed to the party. He was cruising in his new black Maserati Quattroporte that he had copped about a week ago with the music blasting. Future's mixtape stayed in rotation, no matter what vehicle he was in. Phebe was pissed that he made such a huge purchase without consulting with her first. He wanted to remind her that he could spend his money however he wanted to, but he just dropped the conversation altogether. Arguing was not something that he liked and he wasn't about to make a habit out of it. Things were constantly shaky between them and he hated the constant tension.

Keith pulled up to the party and the crowd was thick as hell. The smell of BBQ permeated the air and his stomach began to growl. It was then that he realized the only thing he had to eat all day was a bowl of Frosted Flakes this morning, and that shit had been worn off. Walking up to one of his homeboys by the grill, he grabbed a chicken leg from the aluminum pan that was sitting nearby. Even though the chicken was hot as hell, Keith demolished it within seconds.

"Damn nigga, Phebe ain't feeding you?" his homeboy Luke asked while laughing. Keith just ignored him and grabbed a hot link.

In the distance, Keith noticed a girl that he had seen on several occasions before chopping it up with everybody. She fit in with everybody and seemed very comfortable, so he figured she belonged, even though he didn't know her name. Phebe pulled up about ten minutes later and got out of her car rocking Chanel from head to toe. Her white dress, gold sandals, and jewelry had all been copped on his last run. She was looking angelic, but Keith still couldn't get Cameron out of his mind.

"Hey baby!" Phebe said smiling, as she walked up to Keith and hugged him.

"What's up shawty?" he replied. She rolled her eyes, hating that he addressed her that way. He saw her and laughed because he always did it as a joke to get under her skin, but she had been extra sensitive lately. They talked for a few minutes until Phebe said that she was hungry and wanted a plate. She walked over and smiled at Luke and gave him a hug. Keith grabbed a beer while she fixed her plate. Actually, it was more like Luke was fixing her plate.

"I'm just being a good host!" Luke said in defense while laughing, when he caught Keith staring at him. Before he could sit down, another one of his homeboys beckoned him over, so he left Phebe and Luke to go and see what was up.

Once he made it over to him and chopped it up for a few minutes and was ready to walk away, a female stepped up to him. It was the same female who he noticed earlier. She asked him for two dubs of rock. Keith's wheels started spinning in his head because he mostly only served those he knew on a personal level. Having product on him wasn't his thing, but since he had just left from meeting with the connect, he did have some. Just as he was about to turn her down, one of the homies walked by and the female spoke to him and hugged him, so in Keith's mind, he felt like she was straight and decided to go ahead and serve her.

At about fifteen minutes after eleven, Keith decided that he would head on home since Phebe had been ready to go. She kept telling him that she was tired, but he knew what the deal. Unbeknownst to her, he knew that she was ovulating and trying to get pregnant, which was the real reason she was ready to go.

She cried about giving him a junior day in and out. He could use a stress reliever, so he decided to go ahead and bounce. There was no need in arguing with her. Since they were in separate cars, he decided that he would finally call Cameron because he couldn't shake the feeling that something was wrong. His mind wouldn't let go of the thoughts he had been having all evening. She didn't answer his call, so he sent her a text.

I know I'm probably the last person you wanna hear from, but you have been on my mind and I just wanted to check on you. I need to know that you are all good. Let me know something ASAP!

He figured that was enough to let her know he needed to know that she was okay. They had been through drama, drama, and more drama, but the love he had for her was still there and the thought of anything happening to her was too much to bear.

Keith had been trailing Phebe, so he pulled in behind her once they made it home. After putting the car in park and turning it off, he leaned his head back on the headrest and closed his eyes. He didn't realize he had fallen asleep until he was awakened by his door being opened. Phebe had gone inside and changed into a sexy black piece of lingerie that was designed by Javier Suarez Bordelle. Her pumps set it off. She licked her lips seductively, letting him know what time it was. She grabbed Keith by the hand and pulled at him to lead him out of the car and into the house. Soft music could be heard upon their entrance on the surround sound system. Trey Songz 'Jupiter Love' was playing and when he said, "Girl, you know that you the shh, 'way you walking wit them heels on," Keith smacked Phebe on the ass, and she stopped and grinded back onto his slowly growing dick. After a few seconds, she sashayed off while still slightly pulling him closely behind her.

Once they made it in their bedroom, Keith was trying to figure out exactly how long he had been asleep because Phebe had rose petals on the floor and bed, and candles were burning. He reached into his pocket for his phone, only to realize it wasn't there. Thoughts of Cameron filled his mind and he was turning to go retrieve it from the car where he must have left it, but

Phebe stopped him. She turned him around and unbuckled his pants while getting down on her knees, ready to devour him.

"I know things have been tense between us, but I want to start over and make this a night to remember," Phebe said while pushing Keith back onto the bed and wrapping her thick lips around his dick.

"Ahhhhh!" he moaned, as Phebe swirled her tongue around, then swallowed all nine of his hard inches. She licked and sucked and stopped just before she knew he was about to send his unborn kids down her throat. She wanted those seeds planted inside her, so she quickly jumped up and pulled off her lingerie and straddled him. Making him cum inside of her that night was an absolute must. While easing down onto him, she let out a moan full of pleasure that turned both of them on. Phebe clinched her pelvic muscles tight and continued to ride him like a pro.

Keith always loved to be in control, so he grabbed her by her ass, pulled her closer to him, and then flipped her over, never removing himself from her. He stroked with much force, trying to release all of his pent up frustrations. After hitting her g-spot and making her cum twice, he flipped her over and began stroking her doggy style. When he went to grab her hair and came up empty handed, it led him to thoughts of Cameron. He loved grabbing her hair as he sexed her from the back. Phebe loved rocking short hair styles. Noticing that Keith had become semi distracted, Phebe threw her ass back at him to get him back focused. In her mind, she was thinking that she needed to get back in control because people had always told her that if a woman was on top when a child was conceived, it would be a boy and she wanted to give him a junior so bad, she could taste it.

"I wanna ride again," Phebe said while raising up and causing Keith to stumble a little. He already knew what she was doing and he wasn't about to argue. His mind had drifted back to his phone, wondering if Cameron had called or texted him back. Phebe eased down onto him again and put on a show. His dick was filled with cream as she glided up and down. When she felt him about to release, she leaned down and kissed him with passion and climaxed with him. "Damn, and you wonder why I go crazy over you. I don't want you giving my good dick away," she said while giggling. "I know you put a baby in me tonight," she continued while smiling. Phebe snuggled up with Keith, keeping him from moving, and drifted off to sleep. She knew he wanted his phone, but she wasn't willing to let him get up.

Chapter 4

"I know I'm the last person you were expecting to see, but I need to speak with you and Carla," Crystal said.

"Well, Carla isn't here. She actually made a surprise trip to North Carolina to see Charlotte, along with Cameron," Charles said. "I'm not sure it's a good idea for you to be here while she's away," he continued. Noticing the perplexed look on her face, he hesitantly asked her what was wrong. Kingston ran to the table and grabbed his Skittles and came back watching the two of them like he was at a show. It seemed like he knew something was about to pop off and he wanted a front row seat to witness the drama.

"There is something that I should tell you, Charles," Crystal said with hesitancy. "I... I... I told Charlotte that... that I'm her real mom," Crystal continued while stuttering and mumbling.

"YOU DID WHAT?" Charles yelled.

"YOU DID WHAT?" Kingston repeated like he was the man of the house, while staring up at Crystal.

"Kingston, go in the back and play for a little while," his grandpa told him. Kingston looked like he wanted to protest, but he took off running towards the back, stopping to grab a toy and then hiding out in the hallway. He knew he could still hear without being right there. "What is wrong with you? Why would you do such a crazy thing? You do remember that you are the one who walked out and left her, right? How could you do this without consulting with us? We are her parents, Crystal!!" Charles said while fuming without taking a breath.

Crystal immediately started crying. "You just don't know what all I have been going through," she said while sobbing through tears. After a few moments of silence, Kingston ran up and brought her some tissue, then took off back down the hall. Charles decided to take it a little easy on her after seeing how distraught she was, but he was still pissed off. He excused himself for a moment to go and call his wife.

After calling back to back and getting no answer, he started to get a weird feeling in the pit of his stomach. "Did you tell Charlotte not to say anything?" Charles asked when he walked back into the room.

"No, but I assumed she wouldn't say anything unless you all were together. Did something happen?" Crystal asked. Ignoring her question, he asked her what type of game she was trying to play. Never being asked to come in and have a seat, Crystal finally took it upon herself to walk over to the kitchen table and sit down. Charles just stood there. After about three full minutes of complete silence, she finally started to speak. "I honestly never imagined my life to turn out the way that it did, but it happened. I wish I could go back and change how everything played out, but no matter how hard I want to, it's impossible. I wanted to make peace with everyone before I leave this earth. I agree, I should have come and spoken with you and Carla first, but let's be real. That was not gonna fly over well, so I decided to reach out to Charlotte first. It wasn't easy getting through to her, but we finally had a chance to talk." Charles was getting ready to interrupt her until he heard her saying, "I only have a few months left to live. I told Charlotte about my cancer, but I didn't tell her exactly how much it has progressed. I don't want sympathy from any of you; I just wanted to somehow attempt to clear my conscience and live out my last days happy. I had breast cancer years ago, and it went into remission for almost ten years, but now it has come back and spread pretty much all over my body."

Charles sat there stunned, not knowing what to say, do, or think. When the silence was too much to bear, Crystal got up and ran out of the house crying. Charles knew that he would be in a shit load of trouble for what he was about to do if anyone saw him, but he ran after her and put his arms around her, attempting to console her as best as he could. He felt so bad for her. Blaming her for all of the mistakes in the past wouldn't be right because he was guilty too, but he honestly wanted no relationship with her. Somehow, the news she had just delivered to him made him feel guilty. He stood there while holding her, wondering what all she had gone through over the years and wondering if she had been alone to cope with everything. It took a lot of time, money, and effort to get his marriage back on track after everything went down, but everything worked out and he didn't want to mess it up after all of these years.

"Grandpa, why is she crying?" Kingston asked, snapping Mr. Miller out of his thoughts.

"She's just having a bad day son," he replied to Kingston. Against his better judgment, he invited Crystal back inside and started a pot of coffee. "You can stay here tonight and sleep in the guest room, but you'll need to leave in the morning. Although nothing will happen between the two of us, considering the history, no one would ever believe a word we said, so we don't need this to get out," Mr. Miller said.

After talking for a little while longer and finishing a cup of coffee, Crystal said thanks and headed to the guest bedroom. Mr. Miller and Kingston camped out in the living room watching TV, where they would end up for the remainder of the night.

Chapter 5

Cameron signed on the dotted line for Malcolm to be admitted to the state hospital with the quickness. She was beyond sick of his bullshit. Barely listening to anything that the people were saying, she left all Bertha's information as the primary contact. Now was the time to get away from that lunatic once and for all is all that she could think about. After exiting the facility, Cameron finally pulled her phone out and noticed she had several text messages from her group chat, and one in particular stood out. It was from Keith. Just seeing his code name, 'Kendra' made her heart flutter. Before opening any messages, she also noticed that he had called. *Damn, I wonder if everything is alright,* she thought to herself before opening the text messages. When she read his, her heat melted. He just wanted to make sure that she was okay. *If he knew about all this damn drama,* Cameron thought while shaking her head. She finally decided to call him back because he had called quite a few times before, but he didn't ever answer. It was kinda late, so she just sent him a text instead of calling.

Life is so crazy! You won't believe what happened today. Thanks for checking on me! (smiley face)

She replied to him while smiling and then opened her group chat and noticed that it was mostly Shay clowning and sending screen shots. After she caught up on reading their messages, she sent a text.

Cameron: Y'all ain't gon believe what the fuck happened today.

Shay: Oh lord! What's going on now?

Toya: You didn't even text and tell us when y'all made it. What happened? Do we need to brace ourselves?

Cameron: Shit, I didn't even have time to text. Drama started as soon as we made it. Guess who opened my sister's door?

Toya: Oh my gawd!! You better not say Malcolm…you better not!!

Cameron: YES!! Malcolm!!

Sonya: What the hell?! Girl!!!!

Cameron: All hell broke loose after that! I'm bout to send a voice memo explaining everything while I'm heading to pick up my mama. I'm ready to go back home but she tripping. I'm not staying here tonight though, so she will have to catch a flight if she decides to stay.

After a few minutes passed, she knew her girls had listened to her voice memo because text messages started coming in.

Toya: Wait wait wait!! Charlotte might not be your sister? Or what? WTH going on?

Shay: You leaving Malcolm in North Carolina in the nut house?

Sonya: You shot him? Lawd!!

Cameron: Yes yes yes!!

Toya: It's gonna take a minute to process all of this. Let me listen to this damn message again.

Shay: Me too shit

Sonya: I just don't even know what to say! Like really!!

Cameron: Hell I don't know either! Shit is just crazy!!

Toya: Beyond crazy!

Sonya: Are you gonna call Bertha?

Cameron: Hell naw!! Fuck that family!

Sonya: You probably should call her and give her a heads up though...I mean, that's her son.

Cameron: I might but they need to put her ass in the room beside him.

Shay: So what you and your mom gonna do? Y'all gon stay up there?

Cameron: I'm ready to go now and if it's up to me, we leaving as soon as I make it back. Mom stayed to talk to Charlotte while I came to sign these papers.

Toya: This is just...just...CRAZY AS FUCK!!!

Cameron: Well let me call Bertha since Sonya insisted. I'll holla at y'all later.

Cameron took a deep breath and decided to call Bertha. It was pretty late and she was really hoping she didn't answer, but after two rings, she faced reality that her wish wasn't granted. "Hello," Bertha said.

"Hey, I was just calling to let you know that your son has been admitted into the State Mental Health facility of North Carolina and-"

Cameron couldn't finish her sentence before Bertha started cussing her out. "WHAT THE FUCK DO YOU MEAN? WHAT DID YOU DO TO HIM YOU LITTLE LOWDOWN BITCH?" Bertha screamed.

Cameron just took the phone from her ear, looked down at it, and tried to figure out why she even bothered calling in the first place. *I'm gonna kick Sonya's ass,* she thought to herself. Bertha was still yelling and calling her every name she could think of. Cameron simply told her that she was listed as his emergency contact and hung up on her before she heard the word bitch one more time. "I knew that shit was about to be a waste of time," Cameron said while shaking her head.

When she pulled back up to Charlotte's house, she just sat there staring into space for about five minutes. Going back in there just wasn't gonna cut it, so she dialed her mom's cellphone number, but got no answer. "I knew she wasn't gonna answer... ugh," Cameron said while rolling her eyes. After sitting there for about three or four more minutes, she finally decided to get out. Before she made it all the way to the front door, it was opened and there her mom was. Her eyes were puffy and swollen from all of the crying she had been doing. She met Cameron and started hugging her while crying some more.

"I know you're ready to go, but I need to explain some things to the both of you while we are all here together," Mrs. Miller said through sobs and tears. Cameron knew that her mom wasn't going to take no for an answer, so she told her okay, but as soon as she was done talking, they were leaving and she would drive back.

As soon as Cameron walked in behind her mom, Charlotte was sitting on the couch crying. Her eyes were more swollen than their mom's. In Cameron's mind, she would listen to her mom, but she was not changing her mind about staying. She already had everything mapped out in her head. It was about forty-five minutes until midnight and if they went ahead and left, they could be back home by eight in the morning. It took Mrs. Miller about thirty minutes to say everything that she needed to say. Neither Charlotte nor Cameron interrupted her. When she finally finished, they all sat there speechless. She ended her speech by telling both of them that she loved them very much and nothing or no one could change the fact that they both are her daughters, no matter what. Charlotte wanted to talk, but she knew that Cameron wouldn't be receptive to anything she had to say, so she opted to remain quiet. She knew she was wrong. She wanted to tell them that she didn't sleep with Malcolm today, but it wouldn't have made anything better. The damage had already been done and this one time she was innocent really didn't matter.

Cameron was having all kinds of mixed emotions. She knew that she had been doing her dirt for quite some time now, but she would never in a million years sleep with Charlotte's man. "Mom, we need to go ahead and hit the road," Cameron finally broke the silence by saying.

"Are you sure sweetie? I know you're tired," her mom replied.

"Y'all are welcomed to stay here," Charlotte said softly.

"Thanks, but no thanks. Let's go mom, Cameron said while getting up. She walked out and headed for the car without saying another word. Picking up her phone, she sent her girls a text telling them that she was about to hit the road and head on back home. Then, she sent another one saying that Cameron is actually her sister/first cousin. They all told her to be safe and call if she got sleepy, after they sent more shocked and confused emojis. She thought about texting Keith again, but he didn't reply to her last message, so she willed herself not to send another message right there. Mrs. Miller came out of the house about three minutes after Cameron had started the car up. She thought about how that yellow car had grown on her, but now she was probably about to hate it all over again.

"Well, I hope you enjoyed your surprise trip," Cameron said when her mom got settled, as she was pulling away from the place she deemed as hell. About ten minutes later, Cameron decided to stop and gas up and grab some snacks and two five-hour energy drinks. *I should be able to take it on in with this stuff,* she thought to herself while turning to her thumbprint radio station on Pandora.

"Have you talked to dad?" Cameron asked her mom.

"I saw where he called a few times, but no, I didn't answer or call him back. I'll see him when we make it back," she replied.

"All of this is his fault anyway," Mrs. Miller mumbled, trying to keep Cameron from hearing, but she heard her loud and clear and couldn't help but to silently agree. "Let me take a little nap and I'll be able to drive some in a few hours. You don't have to drive the whole way back by yourself," her mom told her. They both got lost in their own individual thoughts as Cameron glided down the interstate. Since it was the wee hours of the morning, the traffic was perfect. Rolling with the big trucks allowed her to speed, which would knock a tremendous amount of time off the trip.

Chapter 6

When Malcolm woke up, he was in an all-white room and he felt dizzy. There was only a door with a small glass in it, but no windows were in the room. His heart started beating rapidly and sweat immediately began to form all over his body. His breathing escalated as if he had just run a six-mile marathon. He got up to go look through the glass on the door and, when he did, he was disappointed because he couldn't see out. Knowing that they could see inside without him being able to see out made him start kicking and banging on the door and screaming. "LET ME OUT OF HERE! GET ME THE FUCK OUT OF HERE! I DON'T BELONG IN HERE!!" he yelled. Malcolm started thinking back to the time when he was sent off as a child and became angrier. Thoughts if his mom entered his mind. She vowed to always protect him and he was wondering where she was now when he needed her the most. "Somebody help me! Help me!! Mama where are you?" Malcolm said, as he slid down to the floor crying.

He knew that for him to be in a facility, Cameron had to sign him in. It always takes someone's signature and she had to be the culprit behind this shit because his mom would never do anything like this. "This some bullshit," he mumbled to himself. Just when he was about to start kicking the walls again and show his black ass, the door opened and a nurse walked in holding a chart and medications while smiling.

"Well, good morning Mr. Price. How are you feeling today?" she asked.

"I'm feeling like I want to go the fuck home! What am I doing in here? I didn't do anything wrong!" Malcolm said out loud, but deep down, he knew that he should have been in a jail cell for the things that he had done, especially his most recent transgression that he would never tell a soul.

"I'm sure you will, in due time, but we have to evaluate you and make sure that everything is fine," the nurse replied to him while smiling, trying her best not to show any fear. Malcolm began thinking about exactly how he was going to play this out.

He knew he had to be cooperative, but he needed to make a phone call very soon.

"So, you know I'm from Mississippi, right? Can I get a transfer to a facility there because I have no family here? I also need to make a phone call," Malcolm said nicely to the nurse, trying his best to change his mood.

"I will be able to handle all of that momentarily, but first I need you to take these meds," the nurse said. Malcolm hated taking any kind of medications, but he knew at this point, if he wanted to get out of there he really didn't have much of a choice. He finally threw the pills down his throat, washed them down with a cup of water and smiled brightly at the nurse, who in return smiled back at him before exiting his room.

****

After Bertha got hung up on by Cameron, she immediately called the airline to book a flight. A last minute flight cost her almost eight hundred dollars, but in her mind, she would do anything to get to her baby, even though he would have to reimburse her. Grabbing only a couple of outfits and her personal belongings, she jumped in her car and headed towards Jackson to catch her flight that was scheduled to leave at six o'clock the following morning. She could have waited to leave, but she knew she wasn't going to be able to sleep anyway and she didn't want to take the chance on missing her flight, so she went ahead and left.

Bertha made it to Charlotte Douglas International Airport two hours after her flight left Jackson and headed straight for Hertz Rental when she retrieved all of her belongings and exited the plane. A rental should have been ready and waiting for her because she paid online to avoid any lines that would be there. Things went smooth, and she programmed the address to the North Carolina State Hospital into the navigation system as soon as she got in the car and took off in that direction. Deep down, Bertha knew that Malcolm could use a little help, but she vowed to protect him at all costs and she would continue to do so, no matter what. *What mother wouldn't?* she thought to herself.

Upon arrival to the facility, she demanded to see her son Malcolm immediately. "Where is my son? I'm here to take him home with me right this instance. He doesn't belong here! His name is Malcolm Price. I want him out of here right now!!" Bertha yelled at the receptionist, who was only sitting there looking at her like she was crazy. She was asked nicely to calm down, but when she wouldn't listen to the lady in admissions, security was called. They threatened to put her out if she didn't calm down immediately. After she broke down crying and explained to them that she just flew in from Mississippi, they started to relax a little and show her some empathy.

"Ma'am, we understand that this must be very hard for you, but we can't help you if you're not calm. Believe it or not, this happens often. People come here demanding to take loved ones home, but there is still a proper protocol that is set in place and it will be followed. Please, just try to calm down and we will do everything we can to help you out," one of the security guards said to her after handing her some Kleenex to dry her tears.

After about ten to fifteen minutes had passed, when Bertha was finishing up with a cup of coffee, a doctor and nurse walked up to her. "Good morning, you must be here on behalf of Mr. Malcolm Price," the doctor said.

"Yes, I am. I'm his mother, Ms. Price. Where is he? I need to see him. Give me the papers, so I can sign him out and take him home," Bertha replied, cutting straight to the chase.

"Come walk with us so that we can talk privately, please, ma'am," the doctor said. Bertha reluctantly complied because she had a feeling that they were not about to deliver the news that she was wanting to hear. She followed them down a long hall, where they made a right, then a left, and ended up at a door that had the word, **CONSULTATION** written in bold letters.

"Ms. Price, we hate to meet you on these type of circumstances, but unfortunately, life happens this way sometimes-" the doctor began saying until he was cut off by Bertha.

"Doctor, I don't mean any harm, but I just need the paperwork to sign so that I can get him out of here. He doesn't belong here and having him to stay last night was enough," Bertha said.

The nurse spoke up next. "We wish that it was that simple, but it's not. We are sure that you love your son, and we hope that you understand our rules to the facility here. He has to stay a minimum of forty-eight mandatory hours because we were called after hours. We will evaluate him, and it's possible that he will be free to go, but I can't guarantee you that at this very moment. You're going to have to be patient and work with us," the nurse said.

"FORTY-EIGHT HOURS! MY BABY IS GONNA DIE!" Bertha screamed.

"I can assure you that he will be well taken care of," the doctor chimed in and said. Bertha was sitting there, half listening to them explain how everything works there. On the inside, she was feeling like she had failed her son. She told him that she would always protect him. Thoughts of Cameron started taking over her mind and she visualized herself choking the little bitch to death.

After the meeting ended, Bertha was told that she could visit with Malcolm after lunch. Not really liking that news, but not having a choice in the matter, she decided to leave and go get her something to eat. Deciding to eat at Denny's so she could go in and pass some time, Bertha pulled in. Once she was seated and ordered her food, she noticed a woman sitting at a table in the back picking over food, looking like she had been crying. For some strange reason, Bertha wanted to reach out to the young woman. She figured that interacting with someone would help her to take her mind off of her own thoughts, so she got up and walked to the back.

"Hi, I'm Bertha. I know this is a bit out of the norm and I'm not even from around here, but it looks like you can use some company and honestly, I can too," Bertha said. The lady was looking hesitant, but felt like she could really use some company, so she decided to accept her invitation by waving her hand towards one of the empty chairs. "I'm not even from here. I'm only in town for a couple of days to pick up my son and I'm sure you will never see me again," Bertha said while laughing, trying to lighten the atmosphere. "So, what's bothering you? It better not be a man because you're far too pretty to be crying over a man," Bertha continued.

"I wish it was that simple," the lady replied while trying to sit up straight and gather herself.

"It can't be worse than my life," Bertha told her.

"Yeah right! If I ran down everything that I'm going through, it would take us until this time next week and I'm sure you don't have the time, since you're only here for a couple of days," the lady replied.

"Well, I have a few hours and I'm all ears," Bertha replied. The young lady took a deep breath and began telling Bertha about her problems, feeling good to vent to someone she figured she would never see again in life.

Chapter 7

Keith woke up the next morning and Phebe was already out of bed. He was sure she had an early morning hair appointment or something to do that required spending money. As he began to stir, he sniffed the air and started smelling smoke. Just as he was about to get up and see what was going on, the smoke detector started sounding and he jumped right up. He found Phebe in the kitchen trying to cook and started laughing. "What you tryna do, burn the house down? You know damn well you can't cook," he said while laughing. He started thinking about Cameron, once again, and how she made the best breakfast food. She cooked breakfast better than his mom, but he would never admit that to either of them.

Just as Keith was about to head to the car to get his phone, he noticed out of the corner of his eye that it was lying on the kitchen table. Looking in Phebe's direction, he decided not to say anything and start another argument. For the moment anyway. He went and picked up his phone and scrolled through and got a little disappointed when he noticed that he didn't have any missed calls or new text messages. From Cameron, in particular. *Is she still ignoring me or did Phebe intercept,* Keith thought to himself. Phebe was trying to discreetly look at him to check his body language, but of course, he noticed. "You been through my phone?" he finally asked her. Initially, he was going to drop it, but after noticing her body language, he couldn't help but to address the situation.

"No, I just went and got it out of the car for you because I knew it was gonna be the first thing you did. I was only saving you some steps, so you should thank me," she replied while rolling her eyes with her back facing him. Keith exhaled, bit his tongue, and got up and walked over to the stove and looked at the burnt bacon and shook his head. "At least I tried, nigga! You gonna give me some money for my hair and nails today?" Phebe asked.

"Damn, you done spent two stacks since the other day already?" he asked while becoming slightly agitated.

"I went shopping. Didn't you like what I had on last night?" she replied while smiling and winking.

"But, you think me working a regular nine to five will keep your high maintenance ass straight?" he asked.

"I am not high maintenance; I just like nice things," Phebe replied while rolling her eyes. Keith opened the refrigerator and grabbed the milk, then got a bowl out of the cabinet and his Frosted Flakes from on top of the fridge. "So, you not gon eat what I cooked?" Phebe asked.

"You ain't gon even eat what you cooked girl! Stop playing," Keith said. Phebe had to laugh at him because he was exactly right. She tried to surprise him by cooking, but she only wasted time because she burnt the bacon and the grands biscuits, and she didn't even wanna look at the eggs. She started throwing all of the food in the garbage and decided to just grab her something later.

"Well, I'm about to shower and head on out. My appointment at the nail salon is in an hour and my hair appointment is right afterwards," Phebe said while heading to the back.

When she walked down the hall, Keith picked up his phone again, wondering if Cameron had called or texted him back. *I'll try her one more time later on and that's gon be it, shit,* Keith thought to himself before he started making calls to check on his product. As soon as Phebe left, he was about to go ahead and make some moves. Time was starting to move pretty fast because it was almost ten o'clock already. His right hand man, Luke, was going to be out of pocket today, so Keith knew he really needed to gather himself and bust a move.

Phebe walked back to the front about thirty minutes later wearing a Bergdorf Goodman sundress and sandals. Keith could smell the Chanel Number 9 fragrance before she even made it into the kitchen. She had her face beat to perfection in just that small amount of time and Keith couldn't help but to wonder just what else she had planned for the day. Knowing what she was walking towards him for, he told her to grab two hundred dollars from the top cabinet. She looked like she wanted to protest, but decided to just leave it alone because she really didn't need the money anyway.

"Where you going after you finish with your hair and shit?" he asked.

"I'm gonna ride with Keisha to Tupelo. What do you have planned?" she asked.

"Just the usual. You know how it goes," he replied while sending text messages to his workers.

"Well, I'll see you later. I love you," she said while walking towards the door.

"Love ya," Keith replied. She almost turned around to confront him about that because she hated when he said love ya, instead of I love you, but she had a very eventful day planned and needed to get going. If Keith would have been paying attention, he would have noticed that her nails and toes were already done.

****

About an hour later, Phebe was leaving the hair salon and heading to meet her ride. She was in and out because her beautician loved her and she tipped her very well to keep from having to wait all day and night before getting hooked up. Getting her nails and toes done yesterday had saved her about an extra hour or two today, and she needed all of the time she could get because she was ready to relax and have some fun. Hearing a text message alert coming from her phone, she grabbed it, read the message, and replied that she was almost there and to give her five minutes. She was really ten minutes away, but it was all good. It would be worth the wait.

Pulling into their meeting spot, she noticed the white Camaro that was waiting for her. She grabbed her Gucci bag and shades, checked her makeup one more time and noticed that everything was still intact, then got out of her car. After hitting the lock, she headed towards the ride that was waiting on her. "When did five minutes change to ten?" the voice asked. She didn't even give the comment any thought; she simply responded by leaning over and kissing those sexy lips that were calling her name.

"You know it's always worth the wait," she said when she finally pulled away from those lips that she loved oh so much.

"Aight, you gon start something you can't finish." Hearing those words made Phebe think back to how it all began.

We had been flirting around with each other for quite some time, but neither of us really wanted to cross that line because we knew it was wrong. We finally crossed the line one night after a party and there was no turning back. I had actually gone to the party with one of my home girls, but she saw her lil jump off and dipped on me with the quickness. I couldn't blame her though; he was fine as hell. When I looked across the room and spotted a familiar face, I made my way over with my drink in my hand. He was actually drinking some pineapple Cîroc straight from the bottle, so I took the bottle and downed some myself.

"You better take it easy lil mama," he said. I told him I got this and drank some more. I asked him to dance with me because I was starting to feel good and he said he wasn't a dancer. I wasn't gonna take no for an answer, so I started grinding on him.

"Hmm, looks like I have someone's attention," I said, referring to his hard dick that was pressed against my ass. After dancing to about three songs back to back, I noticed someone staring at me and taking pictures. It was Keith's side bitch who acted like she was the main bitch, Cameron. I was about to head her way, but I was pulled back, so I let it slide for the moment.

As the party was coming to an end, I saw the bitch again and screamed at her. We had been in several altercations before, but there was always something or someone standing in the way. This night was no different. Security intervened before I could get her like I wanted to. Being thoroughly pissed off at Keith, I turned around and asked ol boy to take me home after texting Keisha, telling her that I was good. When I made it to his car, I

51

was still pissed the fuck off. I initially thought about calling my friend, Mark, but I needed and wanted some sweet revenge and it was staring me directly in my face.

I leaned over and grabbed his dick and started massaging it through his pants. "Come on ma, you know we can't do this," he said.

"And why not? He's fucking that bitch probably every single day and I'm tired of looking like a damn fool. Fuck him."

He was trying his best to say no but when I pulled his dick out and deep throated him, all of his senses were gone because he was a sucker for some good head. I was in love with his dick instantly. Keith's dick was big and good, but he had Keith by about one and a half inches. I couldn't wait to feel him inside of me. I licked and sucked his dick so good and I had him gone when I swallowed every drop of his cum. We headed straight to the Marriott after he regained his composure. Once we made it up to room 5914, he took complete control and I let him have his way. We both stripped out of our clothes as we headed to the king size bed.

"So, you sure this is what you want?" he asked me. I simply leaned up and kissed him, letting him know that I was sure and I was ready. My pussy was throbbing and I wanted to feel him inside of me so bad. He had other plans first though. When I felt his tongue on my clit, I almost lost it. He was eating me so good; I didn't know whether I was coming or going. As he entered me, I lost it. To say his dick game was A1 would be an understatement. He grabbed both of my hands and put them above my head, looked down into my eyes, and told me I better take the dick like a pro. With a hard thrust into me, I screamed out in pleasure and pain. After a few minutes, I was able to throw it back at him and he seemed impressed. When he flipped me over and started pounding me from the back, I screamed some more and the people next door started banging on the walls. We both laughed, but we didn't let up. I lost count of how many times I came that night and there has been no turning back ever since.

"Now you already know that anything I start, I can most definitely finish, Luke," Phebe said.

Chapter 8

Cameron didn't start to get tired until she saw the Welcome to Mississippi sign about two hours ago. Her mom had slept the entire ride back, just as she figured she would. Mrs. Miller did wake up once and offer to drive, but Cameron told her she had it because she was still pumped from the energy drinks and snacks she had consumed. She was beyond elated when she finally turned onto Miller Avenue after almost seven hours of driving. She looked over at her mom, who was still sleeping peacefully, and wondered how in the world she stayed with her dad and raised his child as her own for all of these years. "It couldn't be me. Hell nah," she said to herself while shaking her head. Mrs. Miller felt the car slowing down and she started to stir in her seat. She looked up and noticed that it was almost seven o'clock and asked Cameron why she didn't wake her up to help her drive. "Mom, you were tired and I had it; we're here now anyway," she replied, as she was just about to turn into the driveway.

"Whose car is that mom?" Cameron asked.

"I have no idea, but I hope we left all of the drama in North Carolina. It's probably one of your dad's buddies that flew in or something; I see it's a rental," her mom said, pointing to the Enterprise sticker on the window. After they got out and she grabbed her bags, Mrs. Miller asked Cameron if she had her key to their house and, with her hand, she showed her that she did. "Good because I don't feel like digging down into my purse," Mrs. Miller said. Cameron turned around before she made it to the front door because she wanted to grab her phone. Keith hadn't replied back to her, but she didn't want to miss his call or text if he decided to do so. She handed her mom her key and went back to the car.

Mrs. Miller walked in and smiled at the sight of her husband and grandbaby lying on the couch sleeping. The tv was on, which meant they had fallen asleep watching it and left it on all night once again. For the moment, she had forgotten all about being mad at Charles, but that would be short lived. The smell of coffee filled the air and she wondered who was in the kitchen, since Charles was still sleeping, when she heard someone shuffling with the pots under the cabinet since. Just as she was about to head that way, Mr. Miller started to stir and woke up.

"Hey honey, what are you doing back so soon? Is everything okay? I called you a couple of times, but you didn't answer," he said.

"It's a very long story, but who is in kitchen, and whose car is that outside?" she asked while continuing to move towards the kitchen. Mr. Miller jumped up and told her to hold on a second with a look of shock on his face.

"I need to tell you something," he said, but before he could say anything else, Crystal appeared in the doorway holding a cup of coffee.

"What in the hell are you doing here? Did you stay here?" Mrs. Miller asked while staring at her sister with rage in her eyes.

"Granny, she was crying and Paw Paw felt sorry for her, so he let her stay. We slept on the couch, so don't be mad. Paw Paw made her sleep in the guest room," Kingston said innocently, as he walked up and wrapped himself around his grandmother's leg. Neither of them saw him wake up. They only heard when he started talking, as if he was trying to keep the peace.

"What's going on in here? Why are you yelling mom?" Cameron asked, as soon as she walked in the house. When her eyes landed on Crystal, she asked, "Who are you?" Cameron was looking at Crystal, then scanned the room while looking into the faces of each of the three adults.

"That's Crystal mom; she was sad and crying, so Paw Paw let her stay," Kingston said.

"You're Crystal? Crystal as in Charlotte's mom that left her? Well, isn't this just great. We drive all the way to North Carolina to find my husband with YOUR daughter, only to come back home to find YOU here with my dad. This family is some kinda fucked up. Did y'all plan this shit? Never mind, don't answer. Come on Kingston, let's go," Cameron said.

"Cameron, watch your mouth young lady. And what happened in North Carolina?" Mr. Miller asked.

"No, what happened here is what I need to know?" Mrs. Miller asked while trying to walk with Kingston dragging on her leg.

"Crystal stopped by to talk to both of us, but, of course, you were gone. Wait, where the hell is Malcolm? Did you say you caught him at Charlotte's house? Where is she? Are you okay, Cameron?" Mr. Miller stopped explaining himself and asked. He knew that nothing had happened between him and Crystal, so his concern shifted to his children. He wanted to choke Malcolm now more than ever, but the urge would become greater at a later date. The room fell silent with everyone having their own personal thoughts. The silence was broken when Kingston said he was hungry and asked for some cereal. No one moved or said anything for about forty-five more seconds until Cameron told him to go and fix himself a bowl.

"Crystal, did you come here because you knew I would be gone? Charles, what would make you think it was ok for her to stay here without me being home, considering your history together?" Mrs. Miller asked.

"Please let me explain, Carla. Just hear me out, please. I know this is a bit awkward, but nothing happened. Absolutely nothing at all," Crystal said.

While Crystal was talking, Carla stood there and started thinking back to the last time she saw her sister. She had put hands on her after finding out she had slept with her husband and really could have killed her that day if Charles wouldn't have pulled her off of her. Now, here she was again after all of these years, in her house and had been there overnight with her husband. ALONE! Mrs. Miller's hands started sweating and she started shaking. All she could see was herself choking the life out of Crystal. Just as she began to move forward, she felt some sharp pains in her chest; she screamed out in horrific pain, then everything went black.

Chapter 9

While Bertha was gone, Malcolm was forced to have a counseling session with his assigned therapist. He declined about three times, but was finally told that if he continued to refuse, it would only make his stay longer. He hopped up with the quickness after he heard the therapist say those words. Staying past the mandatory forty-eight hours was not something Malcolm was wanting or willing to do. Calming himself, he quietly followed the therapist to her office.

With his mind set on not saying much of anything, Malcolm finally broke the ice when the topic on anger emerged. "Anger is a common emotion that can help individuals relieve stress, motivate them to solve problems, and provide a way, through healthy expression, for people to discuss their negative feelings. It is normal to experience anger, and at times, anger is the appropriate response to the actions of others. Anger sometimes arises because we unconsciously think of past experiences. What causes you to become angry, Malcolm?" the therapist asked.

"People. People who don't do what I say make me angry, but I've been working on it," Malcolm said, trying to choose his words wisely.

"Would you consider yourself to be an angry person or do people just make you angry?" the therapist asked.

"I SAID PEOPLE MAKE ME ANGRY! DON'T BECOME ONE OF THOSE PEOPLE, PLEASE MA'AM!" Malcolm screamed. The therapist was a bit frightened, but she wasn't about to let him stop her from doing her job so she continued.

"Have there been times when you wish you could have reacted to your issues of anger differently?" she asked.

Malcolm sighed and began thinking about something he had done recently out of anger that he really regretted. He felt like he had to get to someone before they got to him, but now he wished that he could change how things had turned out. He would never tell a soul about what he had done because it would cost him his life.

"Do you have any anger issues, ma'am? Are there things that you have done that you wish you could change?" Malcolm asked the therapist nicely. The therapist was taken aback by his questions and straight forwardness. Being that she had just had a rough couple of days of arguing with her live-in boyfriend, she stepped out of her comfort zone and started venting about her boyfriend of six years not marrying her yet.

She fussed and talked for about five minutes before finally catching herself. Clearing her throat, she tried to regain control of the session. It was difficult to do, so she had to excuse herself for a few moments. "I'll be right back," the therapist said while she was getting up to go step outside for a few moments. She knew that she would have to give Malcolm a good recommendation because of her slip up and she was already regretting it because that was not normal for her to do.

When she left out of the office, Malcolm leaned his head back on his chair and closed his eyes and starting thinking about what he was gonna do as soon as he got released. The first thing that popped into his mind was making sure Cameron didn't leave him. He decided he would buy her more gifts like he did before spontaneously while she was mourning the loss of her brother. *That really made her happy. Yeah, I'll get her some more gifts. Maybe we can build a new house too and have a baby,* Malcolm thought to himself while smiling from ear to ear, just as the therapist was walking back into the room.

"What are you smiling about?" she asked pleasantly while sitting back down in her chair.

"I was just thinking about ways to make my wife happy again. I know I have messed up in the past, but I know exactly how to make it right now. I'm gonna start by asking her to expand our family," Malcolm said while continuing to smile. *I wonder if Kingston is really my son. When I did that DNA test, I told them to make sure that the results turned out in my favor. If we have another baby, it really won't even matter, but I think I'll do another test on Kingston, just so I will know for sure,*

Malcolm thought to himself. Malcolm didn't hear any more words that the therapist was saying; his own thoughts had consumed him, so he was only nodding his head when she asked him a question or made a statement. The session ended about ten minutes later and he went back to his room.

As Bertha was driving back to the hospital, her heart went out to the young woman that she had just let vent to her for the past two hours. "I hope her sister, well, cousin or whatever, can forgive her for her mistakes because we all make mistakes. That boy that's in the middle just needs a real good ass whooping. He just played on her weakness. I wish I could give it to him myself," Bertha said to herself. "Lord, I didn't even get her name so that I can lift her up in prayer. Her entire family needs prayer, but I can pray without calling any names because God already knows," she continued talking to herself.

After Bertha made it back to the hospital, she was told that she could visit Malcolm in ten minutes, so she sat down and waited. While waiting, she decided to call her daughter because she couldn't get her on the phone before she left. When she finally answered, Bertha explained to her what was going on; the little details that she had anyway. Her daughter asked her if she needed her to come, but Bertha told her she didn't that it would be necessary. When she saw Malcolm walking towards the visitation room, she hurriedly told her daughter that she would talk to her later and ended the call.

"Hey there son," Bertha greeted Malcolm with a hug and a kiss on the cheek. "How are you doing? Are they treating you okay in here?" she asked.

"I'll be better when I can leave here and get home to my wife. I have to make things work," he replied.

Bertha fell silent for a moment, trying to carefully gather her thoughts and choose the right words to say. "Don't you see that little tramp, I mean, that girl is the root to all of your problems? I think it's time for you to let her go," Bertha said.

"She's my wife, mom. I don't know how many times I have to tell you that," Malcolm replied.

"Well, she doesn't have to be. She is going to be the death of you," his mom told him. Not wanting to upset him, she decided to change the subject. "I went and ate at Denny's while waiting to see you and I met this poor girl. She said after the day she had yesterday, she couldn't believe she was even out, but she just didn't want to be at home. I hate that she is going through so much, but it made me realize that we all have problems and there is always someone worse off than you. That poor girl just found out that her mom left her with her sister to raise. Poor thing hated her sister all her life for no reason and just found out the girl is her cousin and her sister. Isn't that just sad" Bertha said.

Malcolm had been looking down, but he looked up when his mom said all of that. "What was her name?" Malcolm asked, thinking that there was no way it could be who he was thinking about.

"I realized that I didn't even get her name while I was on the way back here," Bertha said while shaking her head. "I'm gonna be praying for her and her family though," she continued. Malcolm grew quiet as he wrecked his brain trying to figure out if the lady his mom had met could have been Charlotte. "What's wrong baby?" Bertha asked.

"Oh nothing, I'm just ready to get back to work," he replied.

Chapter 10

Keith dropped everything he was doing when his phone rang and Cameron's number displayed on the screen. "You finally decided to call me back huh," he said when he answered, trying to act like he had an attitude, but he was happy as hell on the inside. When he heard her crying, his mood instantly changed and he began to think the worse. "What's wrong bae? Where are you?" he asked. The only words that he could make out were mom, hospital, and Tupelo. He let her cry into the phone as he made a detour and headed towards the hospital. His initial plans were to go check on one of his spots, but that could wait until later on. Just having her on the phone made all the feelings that he had for her rush back and hit him like a wave hitting a surfer. He just wanted to hold her in his arms and never let her go. Cameron told him to hold on for a second and, as soon as she did, his phone beeped and it was his dad. He clicked over with hopes that whatever his dad had to say, he would say it and get it over with quickly. When he noticed that his dad was just wanting to make small talk, he hurriedly told him that he was on the phone with Cameron and something was wrong with her mom and they had to rush her to the hospital in Tupelo from Starkville, so he was headed that way.

"Do you need me to drive you or meet you there?" his dad asked.

"Nah, I'm good pops. I'm already headed that way because I was in West Point, but I'll call you back," Keith said and clicked back over just as Cameron was coming back on the line. Keith didn't really give a fuck about Malcolm, but he didn't want to cause any problems, so he asked Cameron if he was at the hospital with her.

"He's at a hospital, but not this one. It's a long story. You didn't get my call and text message last night?" Cameron replied. Keith shook his head and instantly got pissed off at Phebe before he told her he didn't get them. She told him she had to go check on her dad, but she would text him with an update and also fill him in on everything later. After hanging up with Cameron, Keith decided to call Phebe, but she didn't answer.

****

Phebe didn't answer Keith's call because she didn't want him to hear the monitors beeping in the background and have to come up with a lie explaining where the hell she was. She swiped up on the screen and set a reminder to call him back in an hour. As soon as her and Luke finished eating and were heading to the mall about an hour and a half ago, he began to sweat and said he felt dizzy. Pulling over to the side of the road just in time after swerving in and out of traffic, Luke opened his door and spilled his guts. It seemed like he threw up everything he had eaten not just that day, but all week long. Once he finally finished, he looked completely out of it and Phebe was scared shitless by his facial expression. His eyes were rolling into the back of his head and Phebe started to panic. Slapping his face lightly to try to keep him conscious was barely working, so she grabbed her phone and dialed 911.

Thanking God that they were in a bigger city, the ambulance came within five minutes and Phebe followed them to the hospital. Luke had to be given fluids, so he was hooked up to an IV immediately. The doctor said that it seemed to be a severe case of food poisoning, but they had to run more tests to confirm it. Phebe looked at him and fussed because she had told him not to order a rare cooked steak, but he just wouldn't listen. They had been there for over two hours now and it didn't look like they would be leaving anytime soon. Phebe texted Keisha to make sure she was still up on game. *It's not like Keith to call around checking up on me, but you can't ever be too careful,* she thought as she was sending the text message.

Phebe: You know I'm still with you all day today right?

Keisha: Yeah, I gotcha. Where y'all end up at anyway?

Phebe: Girl, we in Tupelo. How about we at the hospital tho. I think he got food poisoning.

Keisha: Damn. Did you ever tell him you pregnant?

Phebe: Not yet. I'm still tryna see how I'ma play this out. I know Keith knew I was ovulating last night and thought I was tryna get pregnant, so depending on what I decide, it could still work out either way. I just gotta weigh my options.

Keisha: You gon fuck around and get somebody killed.

Phebe: The only person who knows this shit is you. I'ma figure it all out though.

Keisha: Well, what about the other situation with Luke? This is some crazy shit y'all doing and I don't know why you still dragging Keith along.

Phebe: You know the plan won't work if I just up and leave him. I still gotta play the role. Keith don't really want me anyway; it's all about that bitch Cameron, so I'll just get all I can before I leave his ass.

Keisha: Well, I hope you know what you doing girl. This shit is dangerous.

Phebe: I do. I'll talk to you later though; the doctor just walked back in.

"Well, the good news is you're gonna live. The bad news is you're gonna have to be here until this whole iv bag is gone," the doctor said.

"And just how long is that gonna take doc?" Luke sighed and asked. He hated hospitals, doctors, and everything similar.

"Probably another three to four hours and then with this prescription, you should be good to go, if nothing else goes wrong," he answered while writing a prescription for a high dosage of antibiotics. After he talked for a few more minutes, he left back out of the room.

"Well, it could have been worse than this so smile," Phebe said to Luke once they were alone again.

"You're right, but who wants to be in the hospital at any time?" he said in response.

"The time will fly by. I'm about to go find a vending machine and get a drink and a snack right quick," Phebe said while getting up.

It took almost ten minutes, but Phebe finally found the vending machines. Someone sent her in the wrong direction when she asked, instead of just saying they didn't know. After she grabbed a Coke and a bag of sour cream and onion chips and was turning to leave, her phone rang. When she reached in her purse to get it, she bumped right into someone while looking down. It was Cameron. "I'm so sorry. I wasn't paying attent...," Phebe started saying before she recognized it was Cameron who she had ran into. Cameron looked at her with puffy red eyes from crying and didn't even know who she was until she heard her voice.

"Bitch, if I would've known it was you, I would've knocked your ass down," Phebe said.

"Listen, you better go on about your business and leave me the fuck alone. Today ain't the day," Cameron said while walking off. Making sure her mom was fine was the only thing she was worried about for the moment. Phebe just stood there looking crazy after Cameron walked off. She expected Cameron to cuss her out and be ready to fight, but she didn't even take the bait.

"Yeah, you better walk off. I know you don't want your ass whooped again," Phebe called behind Cameron, but she never looked back. After she noticed a few people looking in her direction, she got pissed off and decided to head on back to the room while thinking about the messages she had deleted out of Keith's phone from Cameron. *I wonder if she has talked to him yet?* Phebe thought to herself. Seeing Cameron had changed her whole mood and she was really ready to go now. When she walked back into the room, her attitude was clear, so Luke asked her what was wrong with her. She told him nothing, but he wasn't going for that. After asking her four more times, she finally told him she ran into Cameron. Still not feeling his best, he decided to say what had been on his mind for a while now.

"You need to drop that Cameron shit. I'm not about to keep playing second to Keith much longer anyway. We both know this shit is wrong and the longer it goes on, the worse it will be. It's about time to do what we been planning, Luke said.

"So, you don't feel bad about what you're trying to do? Not even a little bit?"

"Do you have a better plan? You couldn't get him to take the job offer and go legit, so I could just take over that way. That would have been much easier, but I gotta do what I gotta do. I'm tired of being the man behind the man who is doing all the work," Luke said.

Phebe just remained quiet, not knowing exactly what to say. She was pissed off that Keith wouldn't just take the job she had lined up for him, but she didn't want anything bad to happen to him. *Damn, I gotta figure a way to make this shit work without anybody dying,* Phebe thought to herself.

Chapter 11

Cameron felt somewhat relieved after she heard the doctor say that her mom had only threatened a heart attack, but they still wanted to keep her overnight for observation. She felt her phone vibrating in her pocket and hesitantly pulled it out and smiled when she saw Keith's picture on the screen. Malcolm had been calling non-stop from the facility and she assumed it was him calling again. When Keith asked her what room they were in and told her he was outside, she started smiling genuinely from ear to ear. Her mother was resting, so she decided to walk out and go meet him instead. Outside of the room door, Cameron ran into Crystal. Not really knowing what to say or how to feel about her being there, she wanted to ignore her, but she told her what the doctor had just said and kept walking. *We have way too much shit going on and it's not gonna get sorted out overnight,* Cameron thought to herself as she headed for the front door.

Just as she made it to the front lobby, she ran into Mr. Edwards. "Mr. Edwards, hi, what are you doing here?" Before he could answer, Keith walked in and asked the exact same question he had just heard Cameron asking his dad.

"Son, I didn't think I was gonna beat you here. You sounded worried on the phone and I wasn't too far away, so I decided to meet you here anyway, Mr. Edwards said. "How's Cookie? I mean, how's your mom, Cameron?" he continued. Keith and Cameron both bucked their eyes, wondering who the hell was Cookie. There was an awkward silence, so Mr. Edwards asked Cameron how her mom was again.

"She threatened a heart attack, but the doctor said she should be fine. They are going to keep her overnight for observation," Cameron answered him while staring directly into Keith's eyes.

"That's good news. Is someone with her? I'm just asking since you're down here," Mr. Edwards said while trying to correct his statement.

"My dad is up there. Oh and her sister is up there somewhere too," Cameron said.

"Crystal is here?" Mr. Edwards asked in shock.

"You know Crystal?"

"Who is Crystal?" Cameron and Keith both asked those questions at the same time.

"How long are you gonna be up here?" Mr. Edwards asked Keith, trying to change the subject.

"I don't know yet, pops; it just depends on how everything is going. I need to get Luke on the phone since I'm away though. I know he said he had some business to take care of the first part of the day, but hopefully he's wrapping it up," Keith said more to himself than to anybody else.

Cameron couldn't resist any longer; she walked up to Keith and wrapped her arms around him, just about squeezing the life out of him. She started crying when he whispered how much he had been missing her. It felt as if all of her problems had vanished into the air while she was wrapped up in his embrace. Neither of them knew that Mr. Edwards had walked off. He was headed to try to find Carla's room, hoping that no one would be in there. After holding each other for what seemed like an eternity, they finally broke the embrace, but didn't let go of each other's hands. "Phebe bumped into me earlier. I was too out of it to even argue with her after she called me a bitch and pretty much a coward," Cameron said.

"You saw her here?" Keith asked while raising his eyebrows.

"Yep, right by the vending machines. She walked that way when she left," Cameron said, pointing in the opposite direction than her mother's room. Keith pulled out his phone and called her again, but he still didn't get an answer. A call to Luke was placed next. He picked up after about four rings, sounding weary.

"What's going on man?" Keith asked him.

"I done fucked around and got food poisoning. I ain't hitting on shit at the moment," Luke replied.

"Word, where you at? I had to get outta pocket for a minute, but I can call the lil homie since you ain't one hundred," Keith said.

"Yeah, call him man because I'm in the hospital, and they having to give me fluids and shit. I'm going straight home when I leave here," Luke replied.

"Bet. Get back straight, homie. I'll holla at ya later," Keith said before he ended the call.

While Cameron and Keith were still talking, Mr. Edwards had found his way to Carla's room after getting her room number from one of the nurses that was at the information desk. He saw a door cracked opened and a white doctor's coat was on a chair. Grabbing the coat and slipping it on, Mr. Edwards continued on down the hall to his destination. It must have been his lucky day because when he rounded the corner, Mr. Miller was walking out of the room with a pitcher in his hand. *Perfect timing. He must be going to get some ice or something,* Mr. Edwards thought to himself. Carefully pushing the door open, he walked in slowly to find Carla resting peacefully. Walking up to the bed and gently touching her hand and speaking softly, she opened her eyes.

"Hey, what are you doing here?" Carla asked shocked, immediately recognizing him, even though she was heavily sedated.

"Now, you know I had to come and check on you. I know we were supposed to end this thing, but I had to make sure you were alright. You know how I feel about you," he answered while still holding her hand.

"I think I'm going to be fine, but you don't need to get caught here or I won't be," she said while trying to laugh a little, but each movement was a little painful.

"I don't need you thinking; I need you knowing. We're gonna be friends no matter what," he told her with sincerity. After talking for a few minutes, Mr. Edwards decided it was time to make his exit. He didn't want to be caught in there, even with the doctor's coat on. But, before he left, he asked Carla if she would make one last trip with him to Memphis weekend after next. She told him she would see what she could do, but more than likely, yes. Just as he was turning to leave, the door opened and in walked Mr. Miller.

"Hello, you're a different doctor. Is everything okay?" he asked, sounding concerned.

"Yes, everything is just fine. I actually walked into the wrong room, but I still got a chance to hold this lovely lady's hand and make sure she was okay. Y'all have a great day," Mr. Edwards said as he walked out.

When Mr. Edwards left her room, she started thinking back to how they had become so close. *Being the charge nurse most definitely had its pros and cons. I had been in the field so long that I enjoyed being able to make my own schedule and being in charge, but on the flip side, whenever there was a problem, I was the one who everybody came to. We had been having problems with our computer system for quite some time and keeping up with technology was a must, so imagine having to write everything down and being responsible for inputting it into the system at a later date. It could be a major headache.*

The current IT guy was out on a family medical leave, so I had to call a new company. I wasn't too thrilled about it, but I needed our software updated so that we could get back on track. After selecting a few companies, one man said that he could be there within an hour, so I scheduled for him to come on out. True to his word, he arrived an hour later. When he walked in, I introduced myself as Carla and immediately began running down the issues we were having. He told me his name was Stanley and assured me that he would take care of any and every issue that I was having. I slightly blushed at his flirtatious comment, but I got my act together quick.

Three hours later, he was able to fix about seventy-five percent of the problems and told me he needed to order a part to finish the rest. Then, he gathered his things to leave. Stanley promised that he would be back in two days and everything would be running like new. Two days later, I thanked him for being a man of his word and for being great at his job. Stanley told me there was no need to thank him because the bill that we would be receiving was thanks enough. We both laughed and said goodbye.

Three weeks later, Charles and I had been arguing so much to where I was putting myself on schedule to work and giving people days off that they requested and normally wouldn't get. I was frustrated to the max with him forcing Cameron to marry this clown named Malcolm. Considering our history, I knew there was something that he wasn't telling me and that infuriated me more. Who forces their child to marry a complete stranger on the strength of a coworker's word that he was a good guy? He never would bend on the argument and it drove a wedge between us that was almost closed.

One day after work, I decided to go somewhere that I hardly ever go, especially alone. I stopped by a local bar called the Dark Horse Tavern for a drink because I just wasn't ready to go home and argue anymore. After being there for fifteen minutes, Stanley walked in.

"Well, hello there Mr. Stanley. There aren't any computers for you to fix in here," I laughingly said. I was three drinks in already.

"No, there aren't, but remember I said I could help with ANY issues," he said while winking his eye and smirking. "So, tell me something about yourself that you've never told anyone before," Stanley said.

While sipping on drink number four, I blurted everything out to Stanley in one single breath... I told him that "I was raising my niece as my daughter because my husband slept with my sister years ago, and she dropped the baby off with us and left her without looking back because my husband didn't want to be with her." The look on his face was one of pure utter shock. All he could say was WOW!! To ease the tension off of me, I asked him the same question in return. I wasn't prepared for what he told me.

Stanley said that "He found out that his wife put holes in all of his condoms with the intent on getting pregnant and having *him marry her, and he never found out about her plans until two years after they were married. He said he felt like their whole marriage was based on a lie."*

That night, we exchanged numbers and have kept in touch with each other ever since. It started out as us giving each other encouraging words. Eventually, it led me to taking a trip to Atlanta with him, where we finally crossed the line. As I was about to call Cameron, Stanley noticed her picture and started having a coughing fit. I asked him what was wrong and was he okay? After catching his breath, Stanley finally explained to me that Cameron was the young lady that was dating his son. We were both stunned! Cameron caught me one time, but she never saw who I was with. I threatened her so bad that she never bought it up again. Stanley and I have been each other's go to person for comfort. We knew our relationship could eventually lead into something more difficult, but neither of us fought hard enough to stop it. What started as a simple conversation grew into a deep friendship that neither one of us really wants to let go of.

Meanwhile, on the other side of the hospital, Luke was finally being released a little earlier than they had anticipated and it made him feel better already. Being confined anywhere against his will always put him on edge and it was not a feeling that he liked at all. While the nurse was gathering his discharge papers, Phebe went outside to pull the car around to the front. Keith and Cameron had just walked down the opposite hall, so she missed seeing them, but she ran right into Mr. Edwards.

"Hello, Phebe, what are you doing here?" he asked, scaring the shit out of her.

Looking like a deer caught in headlights, Phebe stuttered and finally got an answer out. "Umm... I'm... umm... here with my... my friend." She was truly in an awkward position and needed to exit right away, so she hurriedly left without saying another word, not even goodbye. Mr. Edwards just shook his head and walked out behind her. Since his car was parked in the south zone, Mr. Edwards wouldn't get a chance to see her pull around in Luke's car. A car that he was very familiar with and had seen at his own house on several different occasions while he was visiting Keith.

While Phebe had a few minutes to herself, she finally decided to call Keith back, but he didn't answer. Calling again, the phone rang once and then went straight to voicemail. "Did this nigga just send me to voicemail?" Phebe said to herself, becoming pissed off. She didn't think about the calls he had made to her that she ignored. "Fuck him," she said and pulled the car around to the front. Luke was being pushed out in a wheelchair and you could tell by the scowl on his face that he wasn't happy about it. Once he was situated in the car, they headed to his house, where Phebe catered to him for the rest of the day.

Chapter 12

"This shit can't be happening. What in the fuck have I done with my life?" Charlotte asked herself Monday evening as she was lying across her bed with red puffy eyes and a headache out of the world. She had cried so much until she was certain there were no more tears left. She replayed this morning's events in her head for the hundredth time after going to the doctor for her annual checkup. If it had not been for the reminder in her phone, she would have forgotten about it. "Congratulations Ms. Miller, you're eight weeks pregnant," the nurse had come back into the room and said.

Charlotte was so stunned, she asked her, "What the fuck did you just say?" The nurse laughed it off because she was use to all types of different reactions from mothers to be.

After hearing that news, to say she was confused and distraught would be an understatement. She laid there wondering how it was even possible for her to be pregnant. Yes, she knew she was having sex, but it was beyond that in her eyes. After having an abortion, Charlotte received news that led her to believe that she would never be able to have any kids. Even after looking at the sonogram with her name printed on it, with the date and gestation, she stopped by Wal-Mart and bought five more pregnancy tests, with each and every one of them came back positive. Charlotte could only cry and curse herself out for being so stupid.

Drifting back to the weekend, Charlotte thought about the strange woman she met at Denny's. It had taken everything in her to leave the house on Saturday morning, but she had to, no, needed to because looking at the walls was depressing. *Why did I tell that stranger all of my business? It felt good to get it out, but what if everything I said comes back up one day?* Charlotte thought to herself. Her ringing phone snapped her out of her thoughts. It was Crystal calling. She had called quite a few times, but Charlotte never answered her calls. The same went for Malcolm and everyone else who had called. She just didn't want to be bothered. A total of fifty-three missed calls, twenty-one voicemails, and thirty-six text messages were highlighted on her screen.

Once the phone finally stopped ringing, it started back right away. Finally picking the phone up, Charlotte answered with a voice devoid of emotions by saying, "Yes Crystal."

"Have you not been checking your messages? Your mom has been in the hospital since Saturday and just got out on today," Crystal said.

"What? What do you mean?" Charlotte asked, beginning to panic. "What's wrong? What happened?" A fresh batch of tears sprang from her eyes. She immediately began regretting not answering her phone.

"Well, I'm sure it's stress she is dealing with because she threatened a heart attack. They only wanted to keep her overnight for observations, but they ended up keeping her two nights. You need to call and check on her," Crystal told Charlotte. Sitting there stunned, Charlotte began to wonder what else was going to go wrong. "Are you still there?" Crystal asked, snapping Charlotte out of her reverie.

"Yes, but I need to call and check on mom. Thanks for letting me know," Charlotte replied barely above a whisper.

****

Bertha had finally convinced Malcolm to forget about Cameron, for the moment anyway. Malcolm had to stay at the hospital until Monday morning. He almost showed his true side on Sunday night, but he caught himself and got it together real quick. He had actually made a little progress during therapy and discovered the roots to some of his anger. Being controlling had resulted from him being controlled and manipulated as a child. His need to control Cameron was deeply rooted and he was advised to stay away from her for a while. After hearing the notes from the sessions, Bertha was able to convince him to leave Cameron alone for the time being. Malcolm agreed because he wanted to do better.

After calling Malcolm's job for him and notifying them of a family emergency and requesting a few weeks off from work, Bertha picked up Malcolm and he was free. Bertha told Malcolm that she was about to book flights for the both of them back to Mississippi, but he informed her that he would drive back since his truck was there in North Carolina. Bertha had never even thought to ask about his truck and was glad she didn't book the flights in advance. "So, where is your truck?" She asked him.

"Well, I know where I left it, but I don't know if it's still there or not," Malcolm said, beginning to talk in circles.

"You need to call and find out. And remember, you must take your medication every day, okay? I know you don't want to be locked up in a place like that forever," Bertha said to her son.

"I know, I'm gonna do right this time. I'll drive," Malcolm said while heading to the driver's seat.

After driving for about twenty-five minutes, Malcolm turned onto the street where he had left his truck. It wasn't exactly where he left it, but he saw that it had been moved down pass Charlotte's house in the curve. "Who lives over here? I have to use the restroom," Bertha said.

"I have to go in and get my keys, so it will be okay for you to come in," Malcolm replied, not thinking it was necessary to say whose house it was. Not bothering to call Charlotte, Malcolm parked behind her car and him and Bertha got out and headed towards the front door. Ringing the doorbell back to back to back without an answer became frustrating, so Malcolm started beating on the door.

Five minutes later, the door swung opened and Charlotte screamed, "HERE ARE YOUR FUCKING KEYS TO YOUR TRUCK! NOW LEAVE ME THE HELL ALONE PLEASE!!" Malcolm knew she was upset since she wouldn't talk to him when he called. He figured it was because he wasn't even supposed to be at her house the day he got caught there.

"My mom needs to use the restroom and then I will leave," Malcolm pleaded. He was genuinely sorry for causing her any pain. When Bertha locked eyes with Charlotte, she dropped her purse on the ground and covered her mouth.

"What's wrong with you, mom?" Malcolm asked.

"I really just need to use the restroom," she replied.

"Can my mom use the restroom please, Charlotte?" Malcolm asked her.

"Umm sure, right that way. It's the first door to the left down the hall," Charlotte pointed and told Bertha. When Bertha made it to the bathroom, she didn't know whether she was coming or going. Not wanting to jump to conclusions, she tried to remain calm until she could ask some questions. After using the restroom and washing her hands, she noticed a garbage can full of pregnancy tests. With her curiosity getting the best of her, she picked one up and noticed that it was positive. It didn't take long for her to notice that all of the tests were indeed positive.

"Oh my goodness! Is she pregnant with Malcolm's baby?" Bertha asked to herself.

"Is everything okay in there Ms. Bertha?" Charlotte knocked and asked from the other side of the door. Bertha didn't realize that she had been in there so long. She was in there thinking about what Malcolm's life would be like if he and Charlotte got together, or if he would have met her first.

"Yes, I'll be right out," she replied while turning the water on to act like she was washing her hands.

"It's not what you think," Charlotte said, as soon as Bertha opened the door.

"Don't lie to me. I understand that we both thought we would never see each other again, but it really is a small world I see," Bertha said. Charlotte just dropped her head. She stood there, refusing to shed anymore tears. She had talked to her mom and really wanted to go to Mississippi to see her, even though she told her making the trip wasn't necessary. Charlotte had spilled her guts to Bertha and now she was embarrassed and just wanted them to leave. "So, are you going to tell Malcolm that you're pregnant with his baby?" Bertha asked. Charlotte wanted to die right then and there because she realized Bertha must have looked in the trash can and saw all of the tests she had taken.

Damn, why didn't I just take the doctors word for it any damn way? Wasted money on all of those damn test, Charlotte thought to herself. "Please don't say anything about this. I have way too much going on at the moment. I will deal with this at a later date," Charlotte pleaded.

"What y'all doing back there?" Malcolm yelled from the front of the house. Neither of them answered; they just stood there and stared at each other.

"Don't kill my grandbaby," Bertha said and walked off. After getting his truck keys, Malcolm and Bertha quietly left with Charlotte standing in the doorway.

"What were y'all two talking about?" Malcolm asked his mom.

"Oh, it was nothing important, for the moment. She seems like a really nice girl," Bertha replied. Bertha had never met Charlotte or seen her before the day at Denny's but she wished that she had. They said their goodbyes and walked out the door. Malcolm followed his mom to drop the rental car back off at the airport and then they hit the highway heading to Mississippi.

Chapter 13

After Cameron helped get her mom settled at home, she finally decided to go on home herself. She had called in to work for the day, but was planning to return the next day since her mom was out of the hospital and at home resting. Relaxing in a hot, much needed bubble bath with a glass of wine, Cameron started reflecting back on everything that happened. After telling Keith everything that had been going on once, he had her to repeat the story again because he couldn't believe the exact details. He held her tight as she cried and poured her heart out to him. When she finished, Keith lifted her chin and kissed her soft and sensually. She broke the kiss because she started getting wet. The fire between her legs would need to be put out if they continued, and sex had been the last thing on her mind lately. Just being near him had done her heart so much justice. She had sent her girls text messages with updates, but had failed to reply to any of the messages, so that was on her agenda to do as soon as she got out of the tub.

When she got out and was lying across the bed comfortably in her robe, she grabbed her phone and started texting.

Cameron: I know I have been in and out, mostly out and that's because it's been CRAZY, but thanks for y'all prayers. My mom is out of the hospital and at home resting. This whole weekend seems like a movie, actually my whole life does...smh

Toya: No thanks needed girl! Thank God she's OK!

Shay: I'm glad she's doing better and you're welcome!

Sonya: Yes, thank God she is better!

Cameron: As y'all can see, drama is always in the mix

Shay: Oh lord

Toya: Let me brace myself...lawd! I'm not sure how much more I can take!

Cameron: I don't know where to start. First off, I saw Phebe at the hospital. She tried to get a reaction out of me, but my ass wasn't on her. I was worried about my mom and making sure she was getting better and receiving the proper care.

Shay: What the hell did she say?

Cameron: She bumped into me and called me a bitch after she had apologized and realized it was me.

Sonya: Y'all didn't cut up in the hospital did you? Please say no...please say no

Cameron: Nah, I walked away, but she tried it. If we would have been anywhere else under different circumstances tho....

Sonya: That was good. Don't entertain all that foolishness

Toya: Yeah, you had to be really worried to walk away, but I'm glad you did. You're growing up (smiley face)

Cameron: I'm trying! Check this out though, I have no idea who she was with, but I think it was Keith's homeboy Luke. When he was beside me, Keith called Phebe, but she never answered. When he called Luke, Luke told Keith that he was at the hospital. Now, why would those two mysteriously be at a hospital at the same time? I even saw Luke's car out front.

Toya: Wait a minute!! Keith was at the hospital? You think Phebe fucking Luke? Damn that's fucked up.

Shay: Well damn. If that's true, then she's really one foul bitch.

Sonya: Did you tell Keith?

Cameron: I told him I saw her, but I didn't share my thoughts. I was too busy telling him my drama, but I can tell he suspected something by a few comments he made.

Toya: Wait, wasn't Luke at the chocolate party that night too?

Cameron: Yep, but check this out. Keith's daddy showed up at the hospital and we really can't figure out why.

Shay: What the hell?

Sonya: *confused face*

Toya: Oh, you know why? You remember that time you saw your mom with that man and thought it was Stanley? Think back...

Cameron: You think my mom having an affair with Stanley? Ain't no way! He said he was checking on Keith though.

Shay: Lord lord lord!

Sonya: I'm laughing because I really don't know what to say

Toya: Where is Malcolm?

Cameron: He hasn't called since Saturday. I'm having some divorce papers drawn up this week. I can't take this shit anymore

Shay: Have you talked to Charlotte?

Cameron: Nope. I don't even know what to say to her really.

Toya: Well, you be careful. Malcolm is a nutcase. Not trying to scare you, but watch your back at all times and be careful with Keith. All of this shit sounds messy and I would hate for it to get any uglier.

Cameron: I'm glad to have Keith as a friend, but sex hasn't been on my mind, but I'll be careful. I just hope that Malcolm will go away peacefully.

Sonya: Are you working tomorrow?

Cameron: Yep, I'll be there. I'm preparing myself now. I'll talk to y'all later.

The next day, Cameron decided to fix herself up on the outside, with hopes that she would begin to feel better on the inside. She hadn't applied any makeup in quite some time, so she got up in time to beat her face and she smiled at her work when she finished. Picking out a peach colored sleeveless Jessica Simpson blouse, some white slacks, and nude Jessica Simpson heels, she started feeling better already. The new jewelry she put on set the entire outfit off and made her look like a million bucks. Leaving in time to stop by and check on her mom, she headed out the door. Kingston stayed with her parents last night, so she didn't have to get him dressed. Kingston asked her a lot of questions and even told her he saw granny number two at McDonald's. *I'm gonna have to have a good talk with his little grown ass,* Cameron had thought to herself. Satisfied that her mom was doing fine, she left and headed to work.

Making it to work, Cameron had documents piled up to the max, just like she figured it would be. She had seriously been thinking about taking a leave of absence, but sitting at home every day would only drive her crazy, so she pushed the thought out of her mind. It would be a lie if she said she wasn't worried about Malcolm because he was just too quiet and that wasn't like him. Three days had passed since she heard from him. Yesterday, she called the hospital to see if he was still there, but since Bertha was listed as his primary emergency contact, they wouldn't give her any information. *Shit, I wasn't even thinking that far in advance,* Cameron thought to herself, somewhat frustrated because she couldn't get the info she so desperately needed.

The end of the day came and Cameron hadn't taken a lunch. It was worth it because she had caught up on everything in just one day. At ten minutes after five, Sonya peeked her head in the door and asked her if she was planning on spending the night at the office. "Girl, time really flies when you're swamped with work. Aren't you mighty pretty today," Cameron said while smiling when she finally looked up at Sonya. She was wearing a cream colored blazer and pencil skirt with a brown cami she had ordered from House of Marbury.

"Thank you, honey; you look pretty yourself," Sonya said as she noticed Cameron's outfit while she was getting up. They walked out together and Cameron started expressing some of her feelings of worry to Sonya. Being very attentive and speaking when Cameron was finished, Sonya told Cameron that her feelings were normal and she understood them. Then, Sonya shared a story with her about a stalker she had in the past. They chatted and once they made it to Cameron's car, there was a note on her windshield. Noticing Cameron's shock, Sonya decided to pick up the note and read it. **I MISS YOU** is what the note said. They both figured it was from Malcolm, but Sonya tried to deescalate the situation by saying, "maybe it's from Keith." It didn't work because they both knew that was a bunch of bull.

"Dammit, I knew it has been too quiet. This is some bullshit," Cameron said while looking around, trying to check the surroundings. "I'm gonna have to figure out a plan. I'm not about to live my life in fear," she continued. Sonya tried her best to give Cameron some encouraging words, but nothing really helped. Sonya told her to please call or text later on, and they finally left the parking lot.

After Cameron stopped by her parents' house and checked on her mom, ate, and got Kingston, they headed on home. In the morning, Kingston would be dropped back off there since he was still out of school for the summer, but Cameron didn't want to be home alone at night. "Mommy, where is daddy?" Kingston asked before they got out of the car.

"I don't know baby," she replied. When they made it to the front door, a piece of paper was inside of the screen door and an uneasy feeling came over Cameron. She began fidgeting and looking around. Once she finally grabbed the note, opened the door, and went inside, Cameron immediately went from room to room, looking to make sure no one was in there. "What's wrong mommy?" Kingston asked while following her from room to room. Satisfied that they were alone, she went back and locked the front door and picked the note up off of the couch.

I was advised by my therapist to spend some time with myself and work on my anger and I will try do that, but I have NO plans on living the rest of my life without you. Don't do anything to make me act crazy; I'm trying to put my crazy ways

behind me. You might not see me, but I will always see you, so
BE GOOD!

There was no name on the letter, but it didn't take a rocket scientist to figure out it was Malcolm. Feeling defeated, Cameron plopped down onto the couch and started crying. "How did he get out so fast?" Cameron asked herself.

"What's wrong mommy? Don't cry!" Kingston said, crawling onto her lap and wiping her tears away. Cameron tried to gather herself, so she started tickling Kingston and he laughed uncontrollably. After five minutes of laughing, Cameron sat up straight and told Kingston that she loved, him no matter what, always and forever. "I love you too mommy! Always and forever!" he replied. "Now, can I have some ice cream?" he continued, while smiling.

"Sure, go get you some," she replied while grabbing her phone. She took a picture of the note that was on the door when she got home and sent them to the group chat.

Toya: Damn, he's out already?

Sonya: So, he left two notes in one day. OMG!

Shay: Two? What did the other one say?

Cameron: There was a note on my windshield when we walked out to the parking lot after work earlier. It said I MISS YOU!

Toya: You need to take those notes to the police to start a paper trail. We can't put anything past that fool and this needs to be documented. Something can be done.

Sonya: I agree with Toya. File a restraining order and if you're serious about getting a divorce, go ahead and get the paperwork started. The sooner the better. Since you finally admitted that it was him who ran you off the road, it should help with keeping him away from you.

Cameron: I will do all of that, but y'all...in the meantime, I need to be coming up with a plan. I refuse to keep living like this. I can't text what I'm thinking. I know y'all think I'm crazy and love drama, but this life I live is

hard. I'm gonna get it together; I just don't wanna die trying. Is everyone free tomorrow for lunch? I can explain my thoughts better in person.

Toya: Yeah, I can adjust my schedule. It won't be a problem. What time you thinking?

Shay: I'm free, tomorrow is a paperwork day for me, so I can leave whenever.

Sonya: I'm available. I have a meeting at nine, but it shouldn't last more than ninety minutes or so. It's a follow-up to a case that I should win with ease.

Cameron: Well, let's meet at Oby's at 11:30. I'll get the booth that's all the way in the back.

Toya: Do we need to wear all black? LOL

Cameron: Not tomorrow. Maybe another day.

Shay: Well damn!

Toya: You know I'm down for whatever! I gotcha back boo!

Sonya: It's going to be OK Cam, try to get you some rest tonight.

Cameron stopped texting when a call came through from Keith. He became irate when she told him about the notes. He offered to come over, but she assured him that they were fine for the night. In her mind, she was tired of the back and forth and didn't want to have Kingston in the middle of anymore drama. She was really planning to divorce Malcolm, but it was not to be with Keith. A peace of mind was her ultimate goal.

Keith shocked Cameron after revealing that he suspected Phebe was cheating on him. He didn't go into detail about who he thought Phebe was seeing. However, Keith made it known that if it was who he thought it was, it was some grimy shit. He expressed his frustrations about feeling like someone was out to get him too and told Cameron that the situation she was in only made things worse. Cameron wanted to share her thoughts with him about his situation, but decided that it was best not to upset him anymore than he already was. They talked for a little while longer, then Cameron got herself and Kingston ready for bed. He had become a big boy, but she bribed him into sleeping with her.

Chapter 14

On the ride back to Mississippi a couple of days ago, reality of all of the things that Malcolm had done started to sink in. Bertha wanted to confront him, but she didn't want to trigger his anger in any type of way. It was eating her up that her son had caused so many problems and, deep down, Bertha knew that she didn't know everything. She reflected to a conversation she had with him on the way back. "So Malcolm, what kind of relationship do you and Charlotte have?" she asked him.

"She's just my sister-in-law. I stopped by her house because I was passing through the area and was tired," Malcolm said.

"What all happened on Friday? What all have you done?" she asked.

"Mom, I really don't want to talk about it, so drop it, please," Malcolm replied, becoming slightly irritated, and she dropped the conversation. In her mind, Bertha knew that she had to still protect him, no matter what, and that would include keeping him away from everyone in the Miller family.

Malcolm had been watching Cameron since he made it back to Mississippi. He lied to his mom constantly about where he was going and what he was doing. He was ready to get his wife back and get his life back to normal. A plan had been formulating in his head, and Malcolm was almost ready to put it into action. Living without Cameron never crossed his mind. He was only trying his best to make his mom feel like he was over her. *I can make my wife happy. I can't take back the things I did, but as long as she doesn't find out the last thing, she will forgive me*, Malcolm thought to himself.

****

Things with Phebe and Luke had stepped up a notch after she had cared for him so well the day he was sick. Ready to take things to the next level, Luke had been looking for rings to replace the ring she currently had on her finger that he referred to as a Cracker Jack ring. He was ready to remove Keith from the equation and take what he felt should have been his from the jump. *I was the one who really saved Phebe anyway. I cleaned up the mess and made everything and everyone disappear. He don't love her like she need to be loved anyway. I'm gonna treat her like she deserves to be treated,* Luke had thought to himself.

Phebe was wrecking her brain trying to figure out a way to make Keith take the job she had got for him. The offer was back on the table and she needed him to take it now more than ever. Phebe had been taking money from his stash in small increments that she knew he wouldn't miss because she knew shit would hit the fan soon. Still not on board with Luke's plan, she tried hard to get Keith to take the job and go legit, so he wouldn't be killed. Figuring that it was time to stop playing games, she walked into the living room where Keith was watching TV to talk to him.

"Have you considered taking the job yet? We have more than enough money to live comfortably," Phebe said while sitting across from him.

She must really think I'm a damn fool, Keith thought to himself before replying, getting ready to fuck with her head. "Yeah, I'ma gon on and take it," he said and Phebe began to smile from ear to ear. "I mean, the stash gon be gone in just a min if you keep taking from it, so I need all kinda ways to keep it right, don't I?" he continued.

Phebe's smile quickly faded when she heard his last remark. "What are you talking about? All the money I got, you know about," she said. He would have believed her if he didn't know for sure; she was just that convincing.

"Whatever Phebe," Keith replied while tuning her out again. It would be a lie if he said his head wasn't fucked up, but Keith knew that he was the one to blame for a lot of things. Never in a million years did he think things would be the way they were today though. Strategizing twenty-four seven was at an all-time high now. Life depended on it.

Chapter 15

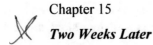

Two Weeks Later

On Saturday, Cameron decided to ride with Keith to Memphis for an overnight trip. They had been communicating over the phone and had seen each other a few times since reconnecting, but they both felt it was best not to have sex. Both Keith and Cameron were stressed to the max and knew that it would be hard to hold up to their no sex policy if they slept in the room together, but they tried.

Cameron started thinking about everything that had taken place within the last two weeks. After meeting with her girls for lunch earlier in the week, she was still pretty much at a standstill about what to do concerning her dilemma. Her initial plan was to let Malcolm come back home and play nice so that she could take him out, but everyone agreed that would be playing with fire and said it wasn't safe. Cameron was still trying to formulate a plan and was frustrated because nothing was coming together. True to her word, she hired a lawyer to draw up her divorce papers and have them delivered by certified mail to Bertha's house at any day now.

Not trying to involve Keith, Cameron kept everything to herself. She had no idea that he was trying to figure out exactly how to take someone out before they took him out. Texting only Toya, she checked on Kingston, since she agreed to keep him overnight. She had taken Kingston's phone a long time ago because she felt like he was too young for it, but at times like these, it would have been good to call him.

Cameron: Hey girl! How is Kingston acting?

Toya: Grown as hell, but I'm sure you already know that!

Cameron: Unfortunately, I do.

Toya: Who is granny number two??

Cameron: What did he say?

Toya: Just that he wanted to see granny number two. I told him I'll have to see where she is and he asked me if I knew her.

Cameron: I'm gonna beat his little ass. Just ignore all that.

Toya: Ain't no ignoring Kingston lol

Cameron: Right! Well, call me if you need me. And y'all be careful.

Toya: We good.

"What's on your mind?" Keith asked while reaching over and grabbing her thigh after she put her phone down.

"If I tell you, you might be charged with accessory, so I'll keep it to myself," she said while laughing, trying to lighten the mood.

"Don't do anything and end up in jail girl," he said seriously.

"Trust me, I don't plan on going to anybody's jail, but anyway, you're pretty quiet yourself. What's up?" she asked.

"I got way too much shit on my mind, so you just take the same answer you gave to me as my response," he said. "We got some serious shit to discuss at a later date though," he continued. He wanted to tell her about what his mom had done the day he took Kingston home with him from Wal-Mart, but decided it would be better to wait.

Arriving downtown, they checked into their room at The Peabody and relaxed for a minute. The business that Keith needed to handle would only take an hour and he decided to do that while Cameron got dressed for that evening. Hitting up Beale Street later was a must, but first, they would eat at the BB King restaurant. Keith and Cameron decided to watch a movie, but the movie ended up watching them as they slept in each other's arms. About two hours later, Keith woke up and got ready to go handle his business. He looked at Cameron's finger and noticed that she was still wearing the ring he bought her and smiled.

Later, after stuffing their faces with some of the best food in Memphis, Keith and Cameron headed towards Beale Street. Cameron knew there would a lot of walking, so she dressed comfortably in a yellow Chanel wrap dress and some gold Chanel sandals. She put her hair up in a messy bun because she knew it would be hot and muggy outside while walking around. After applying her makeup, putting on her jewelry, and spraying on one of her favorite fragrances by Juicy Couture, Cameron was good to go. Keith changed out of his Balmain jeans and dressed in some Polo Khakis, a yellow Polo shirt, and some khaki colored Polo shoes. They were both looking good and comfortable.

The first stop Cameron wanted to make was to Wet Willie's for a daiquiri, so that's what they did. After walking around, taking pictures, and laughing at drunks, Keith and Cameron decided to go to Club 152. They threw back a couple of drinks and listened to some old school jams on the first floor before heading up to the third floor where rap and R&B were played. Keith wasn't really the dancing type, but with the amount of drinks consumed, they were both feeling themselves. Grinding on each other only made them want to head back to the room and that's exactly what Keith and Cameron did an hour and a half later.

On the way up to their room, the two lovebirds couldn't keep their hands off of each other on the elevator. Their tongues created a dance of its own and they were both on cloud nine. Cameron wanted to feel Keith inside of her so bad, but she also wanted to taste him just as bad. She couldn't wait to get inside the room and have her way. Keith was hard as a rock and ready to fill Cameron's inside with his throbbing dick. Bumping into a couple as they were getting off of the elevator, neither of them broke their embrace to apologize.

Finally reaching their destination, Keith and Cameron devoured each other more once they were behind closed doors. "Damn, I've missed you so much bae," Cameron moaned between kisses.

"I missed you too, girl," he said while laughing a little because he actually missed hearing her call him bae. Grabbing her by the waist and picking her up, Keith carried Cameron to the king size bed. She wrapped her legs around him and didn't want to let go. They fell down on the bed together. As Keith started tracing kisses down her body, Cameron started to tingle all over. Keith pulled the belt on her wrap dress and exposed her black lace push up bra and matching black lace panties.

"Damn girl," was all he could say before continuing with his trail of kisses. Stopping at her thighs and biting softly, Keith slid her panties to the side and inserted two fingers into her wet pussy.

"Umm," she moaned while lifting her hips so that he could remove her panties completely. While sliding them down, Keith let his tongue go to work on her. Cumming almost instantly, Cameron cried out in ecstasy and it turned him on even more. After feeling like she couldn't take any more of his tongue, Cameron scooted away so that she could get in the position to taste the dick that she had been missing so much. Seeing his pre-cum seeping out, Cameron rubbed it around his sensitive head. She teased him by licking the tip for a few seconds, then she deep throated him and made his toes curl.

"Oh shit, you not bout to make me cum yet," Keith said while pushing her up.

Entering her slowly, savoring the moment, Keith bent down and kissed her sensually. After thrusting all the way to the hilt, Keith looked at Cameron's face just in time to see a tear falling down her right cheek. Kissing it off, he told her how much he loved her. "I love you too," she whispered, meaning every word of it and wishing that she would have followed her heart years ago. They made love all night long, and if it was possible, he pumped enough cum into her to have about ten babies.

The next morning, Keith and Cameron woke up to a couple next door getting it in. The walls weren't really thin, so for them to hear it, they had to really be going at it. The couple sounded like they were getting enough to last them a lifetime.

"Damn, I'm jealous," Keith said, as he pulled Cameron on top of him. Being that she was just as horny as he was, Cameron climbed on top of him and eased down on his dick.

"Ahhhhh," she said. He cupped both of her breasts in his hands and pinched her nipples simultaneously. Cameron had her way with him. She didn't know if she would ever get this opportunity again. Keith tried to flip her over, but she was enjoying the feel of him in that position, so she stayed on top. Finally getting his way, Keith flipped Cameron over and pushed both of her ankles up on the headboard, causing her to scream out.

"I want you to make the woman next door jealous now," he said, meaning every word of it. A few more deep strokes and loud screams, and he was depositing cum into her again.

After showering together and ordering some room service, Keith and Cameron finally threw on some clothes so that they could hit the road. "I really needed this time away and I enjoyed you. I don't want it to end. If anything happens to me, just know that I have always loved you," Cameron said.

"Girl, nothing better not happen to you; I'll kill a muthafucka," Keith swore. "However, I love you too, and you better not ever forget it," he continued. Keith shared the same thoughts that Cameron had, but he didn't want to scare her, so he kept them to his self.

Grabbing their overnight bags and heading toward the elevator, Keith and Cameron heard the next room's door opening, but paid no attention as they both walked slowly, not ready to face reality yet. They dropped their bags and hugged and shared another kiss as the doors were closing. They heard the elevator ding, indicating that someone had stopped to get on it, but neither one of them looked up until the kiss ended. As they were entering the elevator, Keith and Cameron stood shocked as they locked eyes with their parents. Stanley and Carla.

Chapter 16

Mr. Miller spent all day Saturday doing some much needed yard work. Around six o'clock that evening when he was pretty much done with everything, he stopped and headed to his favorite store. He could go to Lowe's every day of the week. Just browsing around, Charles ran into a familiar face. Not being able to figure out where he had run into her before, he spoke and kept walking. Before he got off of the aisle, Charles heard her say, "Your wife is in Memphis, right?" The look on his face let her know that she was correct, so she said, "So, is my husband," and she walked off.

Charles stood there looking like a lost little puppy for about three minutes, trying to figure out what just happened. A light bulb went off and he finally figured out where he remembered that face from. It was the lady at McDonald's that Kingston had called granny number two. Walking away from his cart that only held a few things that he didn't really need, Charles headed straight for his truck and ended up at the closest liquor store. He had always told himself that if Carla ever cheated on him, he would just have to suck it up and deal with it because of what he had done in the past; but when reality hits you in the face, it's a whole different story. Even without having any solid proof, in his heart, he knew the lady was telling the truth. After buying a fifth of Paul Mason, he headed on home.

It had been a while since Mr. Miller had a drink, so after he drank the whole bottle, he was out. The next morning, he woke up at almost noon with a slight headache, so he took a couple of Aspirins and started his daily pot of coffee. Still undecided on how he would handle the situation, Charles realized that he didn't check the mail yesterday, so he went outside to take care of that. *I'm probably just gonna talk to her, but I can't be mad. I brought this on myself. I can't sweep it under the rug without addressing it, but I know I have to handle it the right way,* he thought to himself while walking to the mailbox. The only thing in there was a newspaper and a letter addressed to him with no return address or name. *Hmm, wonder what this could be,* Mr. Miller thought to himself. After reading the contents of the letter, Mrs. Miller's cheating was pretty much irrelevant for the moment. Mr. Miller went back inside the house and grabbed his phone. Dialing Malcolm's number back to back to back, but he never picked up. Thinking this had to be a joke, he picked the letter up and read it again.

Mr. Miller,

If you are receiving this letter, it means that I finally decided to carry out my plan of eliminating myself from this earth because of the sin I committed. I haven't been able to sleep in months because of what I did. I was contacted by a man by the name of Malcolm Price asking me if I wanted to make some extra money. I was in a financial bind because my mom had just lost her house, so the five thousand dollars he offered me, I couldn't turn it down. I'm not even sure if the story he told me about Fred raping his sister was true or not; I was only concerned with getting that five thousand dollars and sending it to my mom. The only thing I had to do was strike up a conversation with Fred while walking down a busy street. The day that it was supposed to take place, I backed out, but Malcolm threatened to kill my mom, so I felt like I was in a lose lose situation and had no choice but to follow through with his plan. After I pushed him into the traffic in front of that big truck, I took off running and never looked back. I was paid half of the money up front and received a cashier's check in the mail two weeks later for the other half. I know that what I did is unforgivable, which is why I am enclosing the check that was sent to me, and I am also taking myself out of my misery. I am so very sorry for what I did to you and your family. Words can't express my sorrow.

Chapter 17

"I'm pregnant," Phebe blurted out to Luke as they were driving down the highway heading home. They had spent yesterday and last night together while Keith was out of town handling business. He did a double take and almost lost control of the car. Once it registered what she said, he started grinning like a kid on Christmas morning. "Word, well I know for a fact now that it's time for me to make you all mine," Luke said. She smiled, relieved that he was happy about her being pregnant.

"So, how far along are you?" he asked. She told him that she was only a couple of months. The next thing she told him was about how Keith knew her cycle and ovulating days like clockwork, how she faked her cycle and slept with him on a day when she should have been ovulating, knowing she was already pregnant. Luke was a bit angered by her actions, but he told her that he understood and he didn't want any more games. Phebe had no idea that she had accidentally dialed Keith's cellphone and a voicemail was being left on his phone.

Out of nowhere, gunshots rang out like fireworks on the fourth of July. POW POW POW POW POW POW POW!!! Blood splattered everywhere and screams could be heard before Luke lost control of the car and swerved off of the road, flipping a couple of times and finally landing in a ditch. The car behind them timed everything perfectly and exited the highway like nothing had happened, heading to get rid of the stolen car, retrieve theirs, and inform their boss that the job had been taken care of.

****

Charlotte had spoken with her mom a few days ago and was happy that she was doing much better. Her mom told her that she would be out of town from Friday until Sunday on a business trip when she mentioned coming home. She didn't tell her mom, but she was planning on coming home anyway to surprise her since she had taken some time off from work. Not really feeling like driving, Charlotte booked a flight and flew into Jackson Medgar Evers International Airport late Saturday evening where Crystal was supposed to be waiting on her. They had some things to sort through and since Crystal had been staying at a hotel in Flowood, which wasn't far from the airport, it made sense for Charlotte to meet up with her. On Sunday, when she felt like her mom would be back, she would drive on home.

After retrieving her bags and walking outside, she spotted Crystal waiting just where she said she would be. They shared a brief and awkward hug, then headed for the car. "Are you hungry?" Crystal asked.

"Actually, I am. Just stop anywhere except Burger King. It's normally my favorite, but it hasn't been agreeing with me lately," Charlotte replied. Crystal asked her why it hadn't been agreeing with her, but Charlotte just changed the subject and asked her how she had been feeling lately. Crystal knew that she was purposely avoiding her question, but she answered her anyway.

They stopped at Long Horn Steakhouse and fed their faces. Crystal noticed the stressed looked on Charlotte's face and couldn't help but to finally ask her what was going on. Needing to get it out, Charlotte finally spilled her guts about everything that had been going on. She was very honest and told her about how she never really felt a real connection to her mom, even though she was never mistreated. She told her about sleeping with Malcolm the night before he married her sister, about how she had set Cameron up and almost caused her death. Charlotte told Crystal all of her feelings that she had towards her just leaving her, and even about finding out that she was pregnant. As painful as it was, everything was put out there. Charlotte knew that in the near future, she would have to repeat those same exact words to her mom and sister, but it felt good to admit it to someone before talking to them. Talking to another stranger was definitely out of the question after the incident that happened with Bertha. She still didn't know if Malcolm knew about her pregnancy or not, and she really didn't care. After getting an abortion before and being told that she would never be able to get pregnant again, another abortion seemed absurd. Charlotte made a vow to herself to make amends with everyone she had caused harm to and do right by her child. She didn't want or need Malcolm to raise a child; it would only be a constant reminder about the wrong they had done.

Sitting there floored, Crystal knew without a doubt that she couldn't judge or look down on her at all, but she hated that Charlotte had followed in her footsteps, even without her being the one to raise her. She was terribly disappointed on the inside, while remaining calm on the outside. She told Charlotte she didn't know how, but she was sure that everything would work out some kind of way. Being very supportive to her was the only thing that mattered at this point. Hearing that she now had a grandchild on the way, Crystal told Charlotte that it just hit her that she should fight and take the chemo treatments, so her chances of being alive to see her grandchild born would be greater. Charlotte agreed and told her that she would do any and everything she could do to help. They decided to head to the room to relax and continue bonding. There was a twenty-four-hour spa there and they decided that they would hit it up.

Chapter 18

"MOM!!"

"POPS!!" Cameron and Keith screamed in unison.

"What the... what are you two doing here together? OMG!!" Cameron continued. Both of the parents just dropped their heads, not knowing what to say. Mr. Edwards and Mrs. Miller were both standing there thinking about how they had just decided to end things with each other sexually before they slipped up and got caught. All four of them stood there, saying nothing. Neither was in a position to judge, but Cameron and Keith were both silently judging their parents. Mr. Edwards started thinking back to the time in Atlanta when he ran into Cameron and almost got caught.

The trip Carla took with me to Atlanta had been one to remember. We were supposed to end things then, but neither of us could let go. That Friday, we spent the day just enjoying each other. We visited Centennial Olympic Park, Georgia Aquarium, and dined at Sweet Georgia's Juke Joint that night, so we could dance and sip on a few drinks after dinner. When we made it back to the room, we were both sloppy drunk. Holding onto each other and kissing as we made our way up to our room, people pointed and laughed while speaking about how cute and in love we were. I smiled, wishing she was my wife.

We wasted no time tearing our clothes off once we got inside of our room. She told me she needed to feel me inside of her right away and, boy, did I want to be inside of her sweetness. I reached into my pocket and noticed that I only had one condom left, so I knew I had to make it last. She was anxious to feel me and the feeling was mutual, but I decided to take my time and kiss her from head to toe. I kissed, licked, and sucked every inch of her body and had her begging me to stop. When I parted those beautiful lips of hers that rested between her legs and dove in with my tongue, she went wild, cumming almost instantly. I sucked up every single drop and didn't stop until she came again. When I felt like she was satisfied enough, I eased inside of her wetness and I was in heaven. We both moaned

*simultaneously. Everything was just as good and sweet as it was
on our very first encounter.*

*The next morning, she rolled over and wanted some
more. I remembered that I was out of condoms, so I jumped up
and left to go and get some, along with some Advil since we had
been drinking the night before. On the way back to the room, as I
was about to get off of the elevator, that's when I ran into
Cameron. I said a silent thankful prayer that I didn't let Carla
go with me then like she had insisted, or our secret would have
been discovered then.*

"So mom, have all of your 'business' trips been with Mr.
Edwards?" Cameron asked, sounding slightly annoyed. Stanley
snapped out of his thoughts at the sound of Cameron's voice.

"Just a minute; one thing you will not do is act like
you're my mother, young lady. I won't stand here and deny nor
try to explain my actions; let's go, Stanley," Mrs. Miller said,
adjusting her purse on her arm, ready to exit the awkward scene.

"Pops, what's going on? Mom is gonna kill you," Keith
said while shaking his head.

"This won't happen again," was all Stanley could
manage to say.

Keith's phone rung and when he answered it, everyone
jumped because the silence had reoccurred again. "Yo," he
answered.

"It's done," the caller on the other end said.

"Bet," Keith replied and hung up. He noticed the
voicemail icon lit up but decided he would check it later. He
didn't remember missing any calls, so he shrugged it off. They
all rode the elevator to the first floor in silence, wanting to hurry
and put this dreadful scene behind them.

On the ride home, Mrs. Miller was already mentally
preparing herself to admit her wrong doings to her husband and
put this affair behind her. Stanley was a great man, but they both
knew that they couldn't keep the secret love affair they had
going. They had already planned for this to be there last

rendezvous, but meeting up with their children really confirmed it. This was a very dangerous game that they all were playing. Guilt had her wanting to call Charles, but she made up her mind not to call until she made it to her car, which was parked in Winona. Not sure of what it was, but a bad feeling had come over her, and she was really just ready to get home.

Stanley was having his own private thoughts as well. He knew that nine times out of ten, his wife already knew what he had been doing because she treated him like a child instead of a husband, but he was going to tell her anyway. The problems that they had in their marriage had been going on so long that he was sure she felt like it was okay, but things were going to have to change. Stanley realized that having a peace of mind was worth much more than anything in life and he would give his marriage a try, but if it didn't work, he wouldn't continue being miserable.

They finally broke the silence and shared with each other the private thoughts that they had been having. They agreed, once again, that breaking things off was the right thing to do, but they also talked about the good that they learned from this. "Some kind of way, I want to remain friends," Stanley said.

"So do I, but we both know that will be very hard," Carla replied, sounding sad.

"You're right, but we will just see how it goes," he said.

"They were right beside us last night; you think they heard you doing all that screaming?" Stanley asked while laughing, attempting to lighten the mood. She couldn't help but to laugh and blush, knowing there was no way they couldn't have heard with the way Stanley had put it down.

When they finally made it to her car, they shared a long hug and said their goodbyes. Neither wanted to let go, but it was the end of something beautiful that they wish could have happened years ago.

Cameron decided to drive home because as soon as they were leaving, Keith ran a stop sign, so she told him to pull over because his mind was not on the road. Not putting up a fight, he did as she said. Assuming his mind was on the incident that just played out, Cameron brought it up and Keith said he wasn't even worried about it. "I guess everybody got decisions they need to make," he followed up with. Unbeknownst to her, his mind was fucked up because of the hit he had put out on his supposed to be right hand man. He truly hated to do it, but sitting back waiting to be taken out was not something he was about to do. When he finally remembered the voicemail and was about to check it, his phone rang. It was Phebe's mother telling him that she had been a car accident and she didn't know all of the details, but she knew things were looking pretty bad.

"Shit," he said when he hung up.

"What's wrong?" Cameron asked.

"Phebe has been in an accident and she's in the hospital in Jackson. Her mom said it's not looking good. They were almost at the exit to get off in Winona. I can call my mom to see where she is if you want me to," Cameron said.

"Let me think for a min," he replied.

"Damn, I wonder if that was what that voicemail was about. Let me check it," Keith continued. Putting the phone on speaker, Keith pressed the play button on his voicemail icon.

"I'm pregnant"

"Word, well I know for a fact now that it's time for me to make you all mine."

"So, how far along are you?"

"Only a couple of months. I know Keith keeps up with my cycle and ovulation days, so I faked it. I slept with him on a day I was ovulating so that he would think that was the day I conceived because I didn't know what was going to happen between us, but knowing that you are happy, it's time to stop playing games."

POW POW POW POW POW POW POW... loud screams, then the line went dead.

Cameron swerved a little while the message played and Keith was in shock. "Was that Luke and Phebe's voices?" Cameron asked, but not really wanting to know the answer.

"Ain't no muthafuckin way," Keith said. "I gotta play this shit again," he continued. After playing the message again, Keith leaned up and punched the dashboard four times in a row. Cameron didn't know what to say because she had never, in all of the years that they had known each other, seen him this mad before. He let out a loud scream, then kicked the dashboard.

"Calm down baby, please," was all Cameron could manage to say.

"Got dammit! This is some muthafuckin bullshit! I feed these bitches. I have given these two my muthafuckin last and this is the thanks I get," Keith said. "Drive straight to Jackson," he continued. His phone rang and he answered by screaming what, not even bothering to see who was calling.

"Brah, them laws came by looking for you," the caller on the other end said.

"What the fuck they want?" Keith asked, becoming angrier.

"I'll have to fill you in on what I heard when I see you, but that move we made earlier, it was most definitely a must," his homeboy said.

"Today just ain't my muthafuckin day," Keith said when he hung up the phone.

Not wanting to argue with him or piss him off any more than he already was, Cameron bypassed their exit and kept riding down Interstate 55 South. The remainder of the drive was silent.

Chapter 19

Mr. Miller went straight into his room, in his closet, and retrieved one of his pistols and loaded it. *This bastard has really fucked up now,* he thought, as he finished with what he was doing. Calling Malcolm multiple times without an answer, he decided he would just go to his mother's house. *I'm sure she still lives in the same place,* Mr. Miller thought to himself. Hopping in his truck and headed to Bertha's house, tears rolled down his face as he apologized to Cameron and Fred and even Charlotte, for bringing that lunatic into their family and lives.

"I'm so sorry kids. I failed you all tremendously and I'll never be able to forgive myself if I don't make this right. It's all my fault. All I had to do was own up to my mistake," he said through tears while continuing on his route.

After cutting the fifteen-minute drive in half, Mr. Miller was pulling into Bertha's driveway. Tucking his gun in his waistband, he got out and headed to the front door. Looking out of the curtain, Bertha became a little frightened once she realized who Mr. Miller was. She was thankful that Malcolm wasn't there because the look on his father-in-law's face was one of pure rage. Thinking that he was there to bash Malcolm about getting his oldest daughter pregnant, Bertha began thinking of ways to de-escalate the situation in her head. Not giving him a chance to knock, Bertha went ahead and opened the door.

"Hello Charles," she said.

"Where is that lunatic son of yours?" he asked, without even speaking back.

"He's not here right now…" Bertha began saying as Mr. Miller pushed her to the side and forced his way into her house. "Wait, what are you doing?" she asked him. Ignoring her, he searched from room to room looking for Malcolm, but he was nowhere in sight.

"WHERE IS HE?" Mr. Miller screamed, causing Bertha to jump.

"I know he messed up by sleeping with Charlotte and getting her pregnant, but we can handle this like civilized adults," Bertha said.

Mr. Miller spun around so fast that he bumped into Bertha again, causing her to stumble once more. "HE DID WHAT? WHAT KIND OF SON DID YOU RAISE?" he asked with utter disgust dripping from each word.

"Isn't that why you're here? To get onto him about sleeping with Charlotte and getting her pregnant?" Bertha asked. Mr. Miller stood there thinking, not saying a word. He knew, without a doubt, that Malcolm had to pay for all of the hell he caused his family, but he knew he couldn't tell his mother what he was thinking. Finally calming down just a little, he began to formulate a plan in his mind.

"Tell Malcolm to call me ASAP!!" Mr. Miller said and headed for the front door. He didn't give Bertha time to answer before he hauled ass out of the front door, leaving it wide open without looking back.

With no destination in mind, Mr. Miller was just driving. He felt the need to call his daughters, but when he reached for his phone, he realized that he must have left it on the bed at home. Tears began to roll down his face once again, and he started having crazy thoughts about ending his life. *I've caused all of this pain, I'm not fit to live,* he thought to himself. After riding around in circles for almost an hour, Mr. Miller finally pulled over on the side of the road when he saw a road that looked abandoned.

****

Malcolm had left his mother's house about twenty-five minutes before Mr. Miller showed up. He felt like he was really losing his mind because he could have sworn he saw Fred the night before. He kept telling himself that what he did was not wrong because Fred was going to kill him if he would have gotten to him first. Flashbacks about that day weighed heavy on his mind.

I knew I was taking a chance by getting someone else to do my dirty work, but I just couldn't do it on my own. That would have been way too risky. I searched and searched until I found the right candidate. His mom had just lost her house, so I knew he would do anything for some extra cash. Everything was going according to plan until the day before. We had been conversing and I made half of the amount I offered to pay upfront. It seems that he was getting cold feet for some reason, but I was able to talk him into sticking to the plan. I had to make sure he really died, so I instructed him to set a hidden camera up and send me the video immediately. If there was a way that I could have witnessed it in person, I would have but they were overseas.

My guy was instructed to push Fred into the road only when a big truck was coming. It must have really been his time to go because less than two minutes into the walk, a big truck was on the way. I saw the guy laughing like he was telling the best joke in the world and raise his hands like he was playfully punching Fred, then he pushed him right in front of the eighteen wheeler just as we had planned. Fred didn't stand a chance because of the impact and being pushed dead in the center. He was able to get Fred to walk with him because they were in the same unit and he struck up the conversation talking about some lunatic he wanted to kill for hurting his sister. Fred was interested because he considered me to be the exact same problem. I told the guy a completely different story; he didn't need to know the truth.

When my father-in-law called me and told me about Fred's death and said he needed me to come home to help with the women he loved; I had just finished watching the video for about the hundredth time and I told him I would be there as soon as I could. I mailed him a cashier's check about two weeks after the funeral. I will never tell a soul about this and I hope I can stop thinking about it so much before I go crazy.

****

Since Charlotte knew that it would be later in the evening before her mom made it back home, she wasn't in a big hurry to get up. The bonding that she and Crystal had been doing was quite pleasant, and she wanted to continue it. They had talked about so much and were getting to know each other without distractions. Charlotte felt a little uneasy with how her mom may feel, but she needed her to know that no one could ever take her place. She just felt that getting to know Crystal was needed. It may help her figure out her crazy life. She also wanted to be there for her during her time of need. She called her dad's cellphone and the house phone because he was on her mind, but he didn't answer. Next, she decided to call her mom's cell to check on her. They talked briefly, but she still didn't tell her that she was visiting; she wanted it to be a surprise. After finally getting dressed, Charlotte and Crystal decided that they would go and eat at a restaurant that had great reviews called Georgia Blue, then they would do a little shopping at North Park Mall.

Chapter 20

Luke was taken straight into emergency surgery once the helicopter landed at the University Medical Center in Jackson. He had been hit two times, with one of the bullets lodged near his heart that needed to be removed right away. CPR had to be performed on him twice and he had to be given blood because of the excessive amounts he lost. The doctors were not hopeful at all because they kept running into problems along the way and the family had been called to come right away.

Phebe had only been hit in the shoulder, but she was pretty banged up from the car wrecking. She was thrown out of the car and the immediate impact from the tree she hit caused her to pass out. She was flown to the same hospital as Luke for trauma testing. Her blood tests proved that she was pregnant. Therefore, Phebe was able to get the best care in a better hospital and was moved to her own private room.

Three Hours Later

When they made it to the hospital and Cameron parked, she just sat there. She didn't want to go in, but she also didn't want Keith to do anything stupid and end up in jail. He hopped out of the car and took off walking until he realized that she didn't get out. Walking back toward the car, he yelled, "COME ON!"

"Shit," she mumbled under her breath while grabbing her phone. As they were walking, her phone rang and it was Malcolm. 'I guess my craziness is about to start now," she said while sending the call to voicemail.

It rang again, so Keith grabbed it and answered, "Don't call this muthafuckin phone no mo you bitch ass nigga." He hung up and handed Cameron the phone back, like he had only said hello and kept walking. In her mind, she was thinking this nigga really about to flip out now.

Keith went to the first desk he saw and asked what room Phebe Edwards was in. When they told him, he then asked about Luke and was told he was on the Critical Care floor and it looked like he had just come out of surgery. Wanting to look into

Luke's eyes first, he told Cameron to come on and they headed up to the third floor. It was actually visiting hours, so Keith was able to walk in with no problems. Cameron stayed in the hallway. Seeing his friend hooked up to all types of machines broke Keith's heart on the inside, but he wasn't about to let it show on the outside.

Walking slowly up to Luke's bedside, Keith gritted his teeth and asked himself a thousand times, "Why?" When he made it directly beside him, Luke stirred a little. "I put yo muthafuckin ass on and this the thanks I get? You supposed to be my family, but you plotting to take me out and take everything that's mine. I never dreamed you were a got damn snake," Keith said, becoming angrier. He looked down and saw a tube and stepped on it. One of the machines started beeping and he noticed that Luke's breathing changed; he was struggling. He didn't remove his foot from the tube until the machine started beeping louder and he saw a nurse walking towards the room. "If you make it outta here alive, I suggest yo bitch ass disappear because I won't fail to finish the job," Keith whispered and walked out.

"I don't even wanna know what you did in there, but Malcolm has called twenty damn times," Cameron said.

"Fuck that nigga too," Keith said as they headed to the elevator to go back down to Phebe's room. Cameron bit her tongue once again because she knew he was pissed the fuck off, but she couldn't help but to think about her own life. Her plan to get rid of Malcolm wasn't complete and she didn't need to be caught off guard. Making it to room 234, Cameron, once again, stayed back. Phebe was most definitely the last person she wanted to see. Heading into the room, Keith was ready to give Phebe a piece of his mind, but her mother was sitting by her bedside crying. When the door opened, she looked up and saw him and started smiling. Having her mother there put Keith in an uncomfortable position. He was forced to ask how she was doing.

"She's still unconscious," her mother said through tears. He just stood there, not really knowing what to say. After three minutes of complete silence, Keith turned around to walk away. "You're not staying?" she asked him.

"I really don't think it's a good idea for me to stay. There's a lot going on, but I do wish you the best," he said and left before she could try to convince him to stay.

"Let's go," he said when he walked up to where Cameron was sitting. She was more than ready to get out of the hospital. While Keith was in the room, Cameron had called Toya and filled her in on everything that had occurred. Toya was speechless, to say the least. When she finally found her voice, she told Cameron since Kingston was over packed anyway, she would keep him for a few days because there was no telling what else might happen. Cameron thanked her tremendously and talked to Kingston for a few minutes. He was watching a movie and eating ice cream, so he was barely paying attention anyway.

Chapter 21

"We're about to start our roundups in a few more days; the video that we have on suspect KE isn't really clear, but we just might be able to make it work. You were able to get enough evidence on all of the others to send them down the river, but you will have to try to get this asshole KE one more time, so we can ship his ass away too. I don't wanna take any chances and slip up," the DA said.

"It was hard for me to catch him slipping that one time; I'll never be able to get him again," Francis, the female informant, said.

"YOU WILL TRY ONE MORE TIME OR THE DEAL IS OFF!! THIS ISN'T A SUGGESTION, IT'S A DEMAND!!" the DA screamed while banging his head on the table and rattling it. "It seemed like you had a nice little time at that BBQ anyway, so you'll be fine. We will find out what's going on within the next day or so," he continued.

Francis sat there shivering on the inside. She had sold her soul to the devil and, deep down, she knew that she would never be free. Turning her back on her family and even people she didn't know, she felt like it was worth her freedom, so she said fuck it and did what she felt like she had to do. *They would do the same shit to me,* she thought to herself. Getting raided and the cops finding two hundred thousand in cash, a street value of eighty-five thousand in cocaine, and double the value in marijuana led Francis to singing like a bird. Her boyfriend was on the run and honestly, she had no idea where he was so she was on her own.

****

Mrs. Edwards knew that the things she had done had pushed her husband into the arms of another woman. Swallowing her pride, she decided that she would take the high road by admitting her faults, apologizing, and trying to move forward. Arguing, fussing, and fighting were only going to drive Stanley further away. While sitting there preparing a candle light dinner, anticipating her husband's return, her cellphone started ringing. She was pretty much done with the roasted spiced leg of lamb, roasted potatoes, Caesar salad, and his favorite dessert, chocolate cake. He would truly be shocked because he was so use to her arguing and jumping down his throat whenever he walked through the door.

Breaking away from the kitchen to answer her cellphone, she noticed that she had missed her son's call. Before she could call him back, Keith was calling again. "Hey baby," she said sweetly when she answered. He was silent for a moment on the other end, trying to figure out exactly what he wanted to say. Always being protective of his mother, he thought about telling her about his dad, but decided to tell her about his issues with Phebe. She stood there and held the phone in disbelief, thinking of all of the times she had taken up for Phebe, the time they had spent together bonding and everything, and it pissed her off. She knew that sharing her thoughts, at the moment, would not help her son's feelings or mood, so she kept them to herself.

Stanley walked in while she was still on the phone with Keith and was surprised to smell the aroma of a delicious meal and such a romantic atmosphere. After she hung up the phone, he walked over and hugged her. Keith's phone call had changed the initial approach she planned to take with her husband, so Phebe became the topic of discussion over dinner. Stanley was just as shocked as his wife, but knew he couldn't say too much because of his own actions. He made a mental note to call his son as soon as they finished up because the two of them needed to talk. When they finished with dinner, the only thing Mrs. Edwards said was, "Everything that's happened before now is in the past. I forgive you for the wrong you've done, and I hope you forgive me as well. I love you."

Chapter 22

When Mrs. Miller was alone in her car, she had so many thoughts. Cameron and Keith catching her led her mind back to this morning before they left the room, which would be her last rendezvous with Stanley because she made up her mind to really stop before someone got hurt.

I woke up to the best morning sex that I had ever had in my life. On all of our other trips, I usually wake up first and take him on a ride, but he beat me to it this morning. I guess he was hungry, hungry for me. I've heard the expression climbing the walls and that's exactly what he had me doing. I'm gonna miss him, but I must move on.

Breaking away from thoughts of Stanley, she started to wonder if she had ever really forgiven her sister for what she had done. Thinking about the fact that she stayed with Charles and not forgiving her sister had her feeling pretty bad. *I know that it's way past time that she and I talk, alone,* Carla whispered to herself.

As she was pulling up at home, a car had its signal on to turn into her driveway as well. It wasn't a car that she had seen before, but after taking a closer look, she noticed that it was Charlotte. And it looked like Crystal was in the passenger's seat. "Well, I sure wasn't expecting to have a conversation with her today," Carla mumbled to herself. She picked up her phone and called Charles when she noticed that his truck was gone, and he didn't answer. Next, she placed a call to Cameron to see exactly where she was. Cameron informed her that she was pretty close to her house and planned on stopping by before going home.

Carla knew she had just told herself that she needed to forgive her sister and talk to her, but she just wasn't expecting to do it today, which was why she had yet to get out of the car. Charlotte came and opened the door, which snapped her out of her feelings. "Hi mom," Charlotte said while bending down to hug her mother and crying immediately.

"Don't cry baby. It's okay. Why didn't you tell me you were coming home?" Mrs. Miller asked.

"I wanted to surprise you. I hope you don't mind me bringing Crystal. I mean mom, well, I really don't know what to call her," Charlotte said.

"No, I don't mind. It's actually time that she and I had a civilized conversation," Mrs. Miller said while looking at her sister, who was standing off in the distance. "Hello Crystal, how are you?" she asked. "Hi Carla, I'm just trying to make it," Crystal replied.

"Come on and let's go in the house. We all need to talk. Cameron should be here shortly, so I suppose this was meant to be," Mrs. Miller said while motioning with her hands for them to follow her inside.

****

Cameron was headed to her parent's house. She had just gotten in her car after Keith dropped her off. She knew it was dangerous, but she agreed to let Keith come and spend the night with her. Malcolm hadn't called anymore, but she was still scared. Silence always means something, is what she kept repeating to herself. She just felt that he was about to do something crazy. She pulled out her phone to text her friends.

Cameron: I called Toya and filled her in on this, but y'all...things just keep getting crazier by the minute.

Shay: Oh lawd, what happened now?

Sonya: I'm scared already!

Toya: Brace yourselves.

Cameron: Where do I start? Phebe been fucking Luke, and she's pregnant. By him. Phebe and Luke were in an accident together and they both are at the University Medical Center. We caught my mama and Mr. Edwards at the same hotel as us.

Shay: OMG!!!! NOOOOO

Sonya: What in the fuck??!

Cameron: Malcolm called and Keith answered. I'm really kinda scared to go home because he called about

114

twenty something more times after that while we was at the hospital.

　　　Sonya: Wait. You went to the hospital? To see Phebe them? (confused face)

　　　Shay: Girl...OMG!! OMG!!!!

　　　Toya: I told y'all!!

　　　Cameron: Yes. We went straight from Memphis to Jackson. I'm pulling up to my mama's house now. Some other car is here. Ain't no telling who this is. Shit!

　　　Shay: Mrs. Miller and Mr. Edwards tho...lawd!

　　　Sonya: Cam...this shit is beyond crazy girl!!

　　　Cameron: I just walked into my parent's house and Charlotte and Crystal are here. Smh...y'all just pray for everybody.

When Cameron walked in the house, everyone seemed to be in deep conversation, but they stopped upon her entrance. Looking into Charlotte's face, she really didn't know how to feel. "Hello sweetheart," her mom spoke.

"Hi mom, where's dad?" Cameron replied.

"He wasn't here when I made it, but I'm glad you're here. Come have a seat, we need to talk," Mrs. Miller said. The conversation had been going quite well, and Mrs. Miller was hoping that they could continue it in a civilized manner with Cameron there.

"Give me one minute please," Cameron said while walking to the back. Noticing there wasn't any tissue in the hallway bathroom and too lazy to go to the hall closet where the tissue is usually kept to get a new roll, she went into her parent's room to use the restroom. Walking into the room, she noticed her dad's cellphone lying on the bed and wondered why he had left without taking it with him. Noticing an opened letter on the bed as well and being curious, Cameron picked it up and began reading it. After only a few sentences in, Cameron told herself that had to be some type of joke, so she threw the letter back on the bed and proceeded to the bathroom. While washing her hands, she told herself to pick the letter back up and look for a return address. Finding no return address or name, she flipped it back over and started back reading. Halfway through the letter, she started hyperventilating. "OMG! NOOOOO!!" she screamed.

Within seconds, her mom ran to the back and found her in their bedroom holding a letter with tears streaming down her face. "What's wrong sweetheart?" her mom asked.

Cameron fell to the floor crying uncontrollably. "He killed Fred," she said through sobs. It was hard for her mom to understand what she had said, and she stood there thinking that Cameron had gone crazy, so she asked her to repeat herself. As Cameron repeated herself, Charlotte and Crystal were making their way down the hall, and they heard her.

"Fred's death was an accident honey; what are you talking about?" her mom asked while becoming emotional herself.

"What's going on?" Charlotte asked. Mrs. Miller bent down and took the letter from Cameron's hand and started reading it herself. Before she could finish, Cameron's sadness had turned into anger and she hopped up. "I'm gonna kill that motherfucker!" she said.

"What is going on?" Charlotte asked again. Cameron wasn't really trying to ignore her; she was just pissed the fuck off, so she headed towards the front of the house to pick up her keys and cellphone off the table. Hearing her mother cry out from the back, she wanted to go and comfort her, but she only had one thing on her mind and that was killing Malcolm. As she was walking out of the door, her dad was walking in. He knew that she had read the letter when she tried to walk by him without speaking.

"Wait a minute darling, calm down," he said while grabbing her.

"No, I'm gonna kill that sick bastard. He's not getting away with killing my brother," Cameron told her dad as tears started back rolling down her cheeks.

"No, you're not. I can't have you going to jail. I'm gonna kill him myself," her dad told her, meaning every word. "I've already been looking for him, but I can't find him, so we're gonna have to play this smart. I'm gonna come up with the perfect plan," he continued. While they were talking, Mrs. Miller had walked back to the front with Charlotte and Crystal walking closely behind, still not knowing exactly what was going on.

"Is this real?" Mrs. Miller asked her husband sadly while holding the letter in the air.

"I'm afraid so. Did you see the check as well?" he replied. Neither of them noticed the enclosed cashier's check that was on the bed beside the letter and his phone. She dropped the letter and grabbed her chest. Mr. Miller got up and ran to her side. He was still upset, but thankful that he had found out this information before them. It made him better prepared to help them.

"Are you guys saying that someone killed Fred?" Charlotte asked as tears started to roll down her face. None of her previous questions had been answered, but she was trying to put everything together.

"Malcolm!" Cameron said.

Charlotte gasped and said, "Oh My God!"

"I need everyone to come and sit at the kitchen table. We have a lot that needs to be discussed," Mr. Miller said while walking his wife to the table to take a seat. Everyone slowly made their way to kitchen and sat down.

The room was eerily quiet. Each one of them was lost in their own individual thoughts. *I'm killing that motherfucker on visual. I could take everything else he has done, but to kill my brother, nah. He ain't getting away with that shit, and if his bitch ass mama wanna jump stupid, she can get it too,* Cameron deliberated to herself.

Everything just keeps getting crazier. There's no way I can keep this baby now. Maybe, I'm just not to supposed to have kids anyway. Malcolm must die, Charlotte consciously thought.

I can't believe he killed my baby. I've never wanted to kill anybody in my life, not even Crystal, but he must pay for this, Mrs. Miller contemplated.

Lord, Charlotte is already in a mess and now she's pregnant by not only her sister's husband, but also the man who killed her brother, Crystal thought to herself.

"I know everyone has all types of emotions flowing through them right now, but we have to stop and think. We also have other issues that need our attention and to be dealt with," Mr. Miller said, breaking everyone away from their reverie. Everyone looked at him as he began talking. "Being interrupted is something I won't tolerate at the moment, so everyone please remain quiet and hear me out until I finish talking. I went looking for Malcolm, but he was nowhere to be found. I hate that he wasn't at his mother's house, but I know it's good he was gone because more than one person would be dead right now. While I was there, his mother seemed to think I was there pissed off because Malcolm got you pregnant Charlotte."

Looking at Charlotte, Charles asked her, "Is this true Charlotte? Are you really pregnant by Malcolm?"

Charlotte dropped her head and responded with a "yes" in a voice so low that they could barely hear. Overflowing like a river, tears quickly stained her face as she tried to comprehend the magnitude of Malcolm's deception towards her and her family. Sitting directly across from Charlotte, Cameron gasped loudly while jumping up from her seat.

"Sit down Cameron!" Mr. Miller said in a firm voice. Sitting back down right away, Cameron just stared at Charlotte. She was so over Malcolm, but that didn't stop the hurt and pain that she felt from her sister's betrayal. "When we're done, I need you two to talk to each other with no distractions," Mr. Miller said to his daughters while pointing a finger back and forth at them. They both silently nodded in agreement. Thinking about his wife's cheating, he made the comment. "I heard you were in Memphis this weekend," Mr. Miller turned and said to his wife.

Looking very surprised, Carla tried to open her mouth to speak, but he held up his hand and declared that they would have an in-depth discussion about her trip later. He warned her that right now wasn't the time to get into that conversation. Turning his focus to Crystal, he told her that she needed to tell her sister everything that has been going on with her before she left.

"Cameron, I will never be able to tell you how truly sorry I am for making you marry Malcolm. If I would have come clean about what he... and I, for that matter...had done, none of us would be in this situation because he wouldn't even be around. I take full responsibility for every single thing. Because of the relationship I shared with Crystal in the past, he photoshopped some pictures and threatened to give them to Carla one day when Crystal popped up. I really did think he was a good guy, but I never should have forced you to marry him," Mr. Miller confessed, while trying to keep his composure and staying strong. "I did a great deal of thinking earlier after I couldn't find Malcolm, and Cameron, hear me out, but I need you to take him back," he said.

"Have you lost your mind dad? Do you want him to kill me next?" Cameron asked, as she jumped out of her seat again.

"Trust me and hear me out," he said before telling them about the plan he had come up with and making them all promise not to tell anyone who wasn't in the room with them anything. Everyone agreed except Cameron because she was upset on the inside just thinking about having to be in Malcolm's presence, but her dad continued to tell them about his bright idea.

Chapter 23

The next day at work, Cameron really couldn't focus for shit. If it had not been for her paranoia, she would have called in sick. Sitting at home all jumpy waiting on Malcolm to pop up at any minute just wasn't the business, so she went on to work. Keith came over as he promised, but both of them were so occupied with their own thoughts, it was like they were just there. Dreaming about Fred led Cameron to waking up crying, which is why her eyes were still red and puffy.

She wanted to tell Keith about what was going on last night, but she honestly couldn't put the words together. It was still a hard pill for her to swallow. Knowing how Keith felt about Fred would have only added to his problems and that was something she just didn't want to do. But she knew she would have to tell him soon because Malcolm would be around again if she agreed to her dad's proposition. *Why is all of this shit happening in my family?* she asked herself for the millionth time that morning.

"You ready to go to lunch?" Sonya asked when she stuck her head in Cameron's door, causing her to jump because her mind had been lost in her thoughts.

"Yeah, let me send this email right quick," she replied.

"Okay, I'm going to grab my purse and you can ride with me," Sonya said.

Just as Cameron was finishing up, Sonya walked back in and they left to meet up with Toya and Shay at Mi Hacienda. "Cam, I can't even imagine how you are feeling, and I know you probably feel like giving up at times, but you gotta keep moving. Kingston is depending on you," Sonya said. Cameron was so tired of crying, but she couldn't stop the tears from rolling down her face, no matter how hard she tried. "I'm sorry, I'm not trying to make you cry," Sonya said.

"It's not you. I'm just tired. I know I have made some mistakes, a lot of them actually, but all of this just seems so unfair. Have you ever wanted to kill anyone? With your bare hands?" Cameron asked.

"Hmm I've said it before while I was mad, but when I think back on it, it really wasn't anything worth wanting to kill over," Sonya said.

"Well, I will kill for my brother," Cameron said, right before her phone rang. It was Charlotte calling. Trying her best to hold up to her end of the bargain, Cameron answered her phone and made small talk with her sister. Just as they were pulling up to the restaurant, they spotted Toya and Shay parking, and Cameron wrapped up her conversation with Charlotte. "That was my sister... sister cousin I guess you could say and she was just calling to check on me," Cameron said.

"Oh it's cool. That's big of you to try to move forward," Sonya said.

"Let's see if you still say that after I fill y'all in on everything," Cameron said as they were getting out of the car. Toya walked up to her and hugged her, then showed her a couple of videos of Kingston from the weekend. "I'm ready to pick up his little grown ass this evening," Cameron said while genuinely smiling for the first time that day.

They all walked in together and when the waitress asked if they wanted a table or booth, Cameron told her they wanted whatever was available in a back corner. Once they were seated and the waitress asked for drink orders, Cameron ordered a jumbo margarita on the rocks with an extra hit of Jose Cuervo tequila. Shay looked like she was about to say something crazy, but Sonya signaled for her to be quiet. As soon as their drinks were set in front of them, Cameron picked hers up and drank half of her margarita without stopping.

"What I'm gonna say today, y'all can't say shit about it. I can't tell y'all everything anyway, but I gotta get some of it off my chest," Cameron said. They all told her they would keep her secrets amongst the group.

"Once again, where do I fucking start?" Cameron asked after taking a few more sips from her drink. She continued, "I would ask if y'all want the good news or bad news first but umm... I haven't found any good so here it goes. Charlotte is pregnant by Malcolm. She had an abortion before and they told her she would never get pregnant again, but she's eight or nine weeks pregnant. We talked and I'm trying to move forward because I'm over Malcolm's bitch ass. My aunt, Crystal, has breast cancer and it's spreading, and she doesn't know how much longer she has to live. She didn't want to take treatments at first, but now that everyone is trying to move forward and make amends, she is going to start in hopes that it's not as bad as the doctor thinks. My dad knew about my mom and Mr. Edwards, and my mom admitted to everything and agreed to stop seeing him. I'm sure I'm missing something, but last but certainly not least, someone sent an anonymous letter to my dad about Fred's death." Taking a deep breath before spilling the rest, Cameron told the group that Malcolm paid to have her brother killed. Cameron immediately picked up her drink, finished it off, and sat the glass back down on the table. She closed her eyes for a minute and then reopened them to observe her friends' reactions and saw just what she expected.

"Umm excuse me, waitress, we need four shots and four margaritas immediately," Toya stood up and said while still in shock. No one else said a word. When the waitress returned and sat their drinks down, everyone picked up a shot and threw it back at the same damn time.

"OK, that's a valid reason for wanting to kill someone," Sonya said.

"Oh yeah, my dad came up with a plan to get back at Malcolm, but I have to let him move back in for it to work," Cameron said while rolling her eyes.

"What does Mr. Miller need me to do?" Toya asked, serious as hell.

"I can't believe I'm the one who is speechless today," Shay said. "You wanna go see some strippers?" she continued. Everyone laughed because it was just like Shay to think of something sexual to say in order to break the ice.

"This is just too much y'all. I don't know if I'm coming or going. I just wanna wake up from this fucking nightmare,"

Cameron said, as she sipped more of her margarita. They conversed for a little while longer, each of them taking about thirty extra minutes on lunch and then they left.

The second part of the work day flew by and Cameron was excited about that because she was ready to see her baby. Pulling up to the after school facility, she could have sworn she saw Malcolm's car pulling off. Another car looked like it was trailing him and it pulled off a few seconds after. *It must be the drinks,* Cameron thought to herself. When she got out and walked in the building, Kingston ran to her immediately and jumped into her arms.

"I missed you, mommy," he said and then kissed her on the jaw.

"I missed you too, baby," she said while squeezing him tight. "You wanna go to McDonald's and get some ice cream?" she asked him.

"YES!" he answered right away. "I saw daddy, but he didn't come in and speak to me," Kingston continued.

"Where?" Cameron asked, becoming nervous.

"He came here, but he walked back out," Kingston said nonchalantly. "Where's Unk?" he continued.

"I'm not sure, but come so we can go get that ice cream," Cameron said, ready to get away from there. She wanted to scream out loud, but that would have scared Kingston, so she screamed in her head.

Kingston demolished his happy meal in no time and wanted to play before getting some ice cream. Cameron was happy because he was enjoying himself and smiling. While he was playing, she decided to scroll through Facebook and Instagram to pass some time. Everybody was posting memes from a beef between 50 Cent and Vivica Fox. It was quite entertaining and she caught herself laughing. When someone cleared their throat, she looked up and locked eyes with Mrs. Edwards. Not really caring to speak, but not wanting to be rude either, Cameron smiled.

"How are you dear?" Mrs. Edwards asked. Cameron looked to her left and right, then behind her to see who she was talking to. She chuckled a little and told her that she was talking to her.

"I'm okay, how are you?" she finally replied.

"I'm glad I ran into you; I have been wanting to speak with you, but where is my grandbaby? Mrs. Edwards asked.

"Why do you insist on calling him your grandchild when he's not?" Cameron asked.

"Because he IS my grandbaby. That's one of the things I have been wanting to speak with you about. I would like for him to start spending time with us," she said. Cameron sat there looking at her like she was delusional. "Trust me, if I did not have proof that he was mine, I would not claim him. I knew he was Keith's child when I first saw him, but I still wanted to verify it. Keith doesn't know this yet, so let's keep this between us for the moment, but I administered a blood test on him the day he came home with Keith from Wal-Mart," Mrs. Edwards said.

"You did what?" Cameron asked while standing and raising her voice. Before Mrs. Edwards could respond, Kingston ran up and grabbed her leg.

"Granny, Granny," he squealed.

"Hi there baby, with your handsome little self," Mrs. Edwards said as Kingston was blushing.

"Do you wanna eat some ice cream with us?" Kingston asked.

"I would love to. Let's go get it now," she replied and walked off with Kingston.

Cameron sat there numb. Her brain was just about frozen as she tried to figure out how and why this happened. *Did Malcolm rig the test? Did Mrs. Edwards really administer a test? Is this a blessing in disguise? What the fuck is going on?* Cameron had so many questions in her head. She snapped out of her thoughts when Kingston sat some ice cream down in front of her. Once he finished eating his, he ran back to play and Mrs. Edwards started talking.

"First off, I just want to apologize for the way I treated you in the past. I hope that you can understand that I was only being protective of my son, I'm sure you will be the same way with Kingston..." she started rambling off, but Cameron cut her off by letting her know that Keith is a grown ass man. "I know, and I went overboard, which is why I am apologizing now. I hope that we can move forward and have a better relationship for the sake of my grandbaby," Mrs. Edwards said.

"I'm not trying to be rude, and as much as I hate my husband, he is Kingston's father. He had a test done himself," Cameron said.

"I'm not sure what kind of test he had done, but the results I received were 99.999% in favor of Kingston being Keith's son. Are you sure you didn't know this? I kinda assumed you gave him the same initial as his dad." Cameron glared at Mrs. Edwards before telling her that is exactly what she did, since she was so sure that Kingston was Keegan's child, which was Malcolm's first name. Mrs. Edwards was genuinely shocked and pleased because she thought Cameron had been playing games. They chatted for about twenty-five more minutes and they all got up to leave at the same time. "Keep in touch" Mrs. Edwards said and hugged both Kingston and Cameron.

After making it to her car and making sure Kingston was secure, Cameron got in the driver's seat and just sat there in shock, thinking about everything Mrs. Edwards just said. She was in total disbelief. *If I would have known that Keith was Kingston's daddy, I probably could have avoided a whole lot of the madness that has taken place in my life. FUUUUCCCKKKKKK!!!!!* She screamed in her head.

"Mommy, how long are we going to sit here? Are you okay?" Kingston asked, snapping Cameron out of her thoughts.

"I'm fine baby. We're about to go," Cameron replied while finally cranking the car up and preparing to leave.

Chapter 24

Keith hadn't smoked in quite some time, but he was sure tempted with the way his life was going. He had gotten another tip off from a good friend on his payroll and had put a plan in motion to eliminate the problem. He was currently sitting at one of the trap houses, patiently waiting. Throwing food on the grill was an added bonus because people were always hungry. Everybody in the community was stopping by to grab a plate. He hadn't been back to see Phebe, but her mom had called and said that she was awake and should be home in a day or two. Keith didn't provide a response because it would have been harsh and the anger would have been misdirected, and he didn't want to disrespect his soon to be ex-mother-in-law.

Meeting with his lawyer was on his list of things to do. Phebe had done the grimiest shit and there was no way to repair their relationship. He knew he had fucked up before, but in his eyes, the shit she had done went against everything he believed in. Looking up, Keith started to smile on the inside when he saw who he had been waiting to see. His homeboy, Marco, noticed the person at the same time and he was ready to get this shit over with. Francis got out of the car and went around speaking to people, making small talk and acting like she was really there just to have a good time. Playing the role to the tee, she even fixed a plate and ate everything that was on her plate. *Yeah, enjoy your last meal,* Keith thought to himself. When she started making her way towards Keith, Marco did what he was supposed to do and went and hid on her back floor behind the driver's seat. Since they weren't sure whether she would lock her car doors or not, they used a magnetic chip to disable it if she tried.

Making her way to Keith, Francis smiled happily and spoke like they were old buddies. He stood there wanting to choke the shit out of her, but she would be handled without him even having to put his hands on her. "What's up homie?" she asked.

"Just chillin," Keith replied.

"Let me get that same package again," she said.

"What kinda package you talmbout shawty?" Keith asked, intentionally fucking with her and playing dumb.

Kinda thrown off guard by his response, she stuttered and told him she meant the same package she had copped from him before at the other BBQ. Keith continued to play dumb with her and informed her that he didn't know what she was referring to. He wasn't going to take the chance on giving her shit, just in case the wire she was wearing was automatically connected to a computer or some shit. Feeling defeated after about five minutes of talking, Francis finally told him that she would holla at him later. Keith just shook his head, not feeling the least bit guilty about what was about to happen shortly after she was forced to drive out into the country. *Poof be gone, you snitching ass bitch,* Keith laughed to himself before walking off to chop it up with some of the other people who were kicking it at the house.

****

Francis hopped back in her car feeling defeated. She sat there trying to figure out a way to get to Keith because her life depended on it. She was so frustrated that she banged her hands on the steering wheel and screamed. Marco was in the back, ready for her to pull off so that he could get his assignment over with. Snitches made his ass itch, so he was more than eager to handle the bitch that was in the front seat. First, he had some questions that he needed answers to, so he was planning on having a little fun with her first.

"Make the next left and don't you dare try any funny shit," Marco said, as he placed the gun into Francis' side. She swerved and screamed. "Shut the fuck up and do what I say," he said while maintaining a calm demeanor.

"Who are you?" she asked, like he was stupid enough to answer.

"I'm your worst fucking nightmare, you snitching ass bitch," he told her. It was right then that she knew her life was about to end. "Take the next right," he told her, unbothered by the tears that were streaming down her face.

Leading her to an abandoned house out in the country and stepping out of the car, the first thing he did was fire one shot into the air before ripping the wire off of her and placing it in his pocket to burn momentarily. Just in case the police was listening, he wanted them to know what time it was. Francis pissed on herself after he shot the gun into the air. Having no sympathy for her at all, Marco yanked her out of the car and pulled her into the house. Two more of his partners were already waiting inside to make the delivery once they were done. They grabbed her from him and tied her up as soon as Marco made it inside.

After securing her to a chair, the questions began. When she looked up and gazed her eyes with the other two people in the room, she really knew it was over for her because she had set them up as well. "We just wanna know why?" one of the guys asked, who was actually her cousin.

"They made me do it! I didn't want to," she cried.

"Made you? You sure they made you or was you just tryna save your own ass by snitching on everybody else?" he demanded and angrily asked.

"What all do they know?" the other guy countered. Francis knew it wouldn't save her life, so she tried to remain quiet because she really didn't want to admit to everything she had done. The silence was broken when Marco walked up to her and fired two shots, one to each leg.

"Arrrggghhhh!!!" she screamed out in pain.

"Talk now, or this is gonna be way worse than planned," Marco said. Francis started humming like a church choir after he said those words. They all stood there in awe and thoroughly pissed the fuck off.

"We fed you and your family just about all your got damn life, and this is how you repay us? You know what comes along with the game. We all know we're taking chances, but just because you got caught up doesn't give a nigga the right to fucking snitch on the next man. Since you like talking so fucking much, we will be sure to leave a gift for them punk muthafuckas you was working for," her cousin said right before walking up to her and punching the hell out of her. The other guy came up next and swung his Smith and Wesson blade, chopping her head off in one swift motion.

After they all talked for a few minutes and finalized the rest of their plans, all of the men wiped everything down and dipped. Leaving her body there, her cousin took her head and tongue so it could be sent via special delivery, right to the DA. Neither of them felt bad about what they had done. *I should've handled Luke and Phebe this exact same way,* Marco jokingly reminisced.

Chapter 25

Phebe's mom was beyond angry that Keith had not been by her daughter's side in her time of need. She would call him to give updates and he answered, but he was never enthused with her progress nor did he ever make the phone call to her or visit. When she asked him what was going on, Keith told her he would be glad to let her know in due time, but Phebe should be the one to inform her. She sent him a text earlier this morning letting him know that Phebe was being discharged and he replied okay. After receiving the simple response, she couldn't comprehend what the hell was going on between Phebe and Keith to cause him to be so distant with her daughter. *"I will give Phebe time to recuperate at home, but we will definitely be having a conversation about the problems with her marriage,"* her mom quietly admitted. *"This just doesn't make any damn sense for a husband not be by his wife's side after having an accident."* All she could do was shake her head and proceed to get Phebe's things together to go home.

It wasn't until it was time to go that Phebe's mom picked up on what was really going on. Instead of making her way towards the exit, Phebe went to the information desk and inquired about Luke, stating that she was his fiancé. Once she found out what room he was in, she made her way there in a hurry. He was now in a regular room, and Phebe didn't plan on leaving his side. She knew she owed Keith an explanation, but knowing that he could have caused her death, she wasn't ready to face him. Sure, the hit was supposed to have been for Luke, but in her eyes, it didn't really matter. She knew that her marriage was over.

Luke was awake and making great progress when she walked in. He smiled a little when he saw her. She smiled back at him and went right to his bedside and leaned over and kissed him softly on the lips. Phebe's mom walked in behind her; she was just standing there speechless. "OMG, you're gonna be okay. This is all my fault... I'm so sorry," Phebe said through teary eyes. Unable to stop her tears from flowing, Phebe sobbed uncontrollably while trying to comfort Luke.

"Shhh, don't cry. This is my fault, but we both gonna be okay. Things are looking pretty good for me. We gonna just relocate when I get up outta here," Luke said while trying to reach up and wipe her tears away.

"Oh yeah, and where the fuck y'all going to?" Keith asked, as soon as he busted through the door. The room fell completely silent. "Don't stop talking now. Do I need to go back out of the room so y'all can finish y'all bullshit conversation?" Keith asked while looking back at the door. Everyone still remained quiet. "So, now the cat got y'all muthafuckin' tongues huh. Y'all were just choppin it up," he continued talking while shaking his head.

"Now is not the time or place for this Keith," Phebe said.

"Why not? We all here," Keith responded.

"Keith, I don't know what all is going on, but this really isn't the right time or place," Phebe's mom spoke up while walking towards Keith to keep him from moving closer to the bed.

"Did you tell your mom that she's about to be a grandmother, Phebe?" Keith asked her.

"Well, that's great news. I know she has wanted to give you a son," her mother said to Keith.

"No Ms. Brown, THEY are about to have a baby," Keith said while pointing at Phebe and Luke. Phebe was standing there in awe and disbelief. Not knowing how he knew so much, she decided to talk and see exactly how much he knew.

"What are you talking about Keith?" she asked.

"Oh, you really wanna know?" he asked while pulling out his phone. He hit his voicemail button and put the phone on speaker. When Phebe heard the conversation she and Luke were having right before the shooting, she knew that he knew everything.

"Look, I didn't mean for this to happen..." Luke started saying. Just hearing him trying to apologize set Keith off, and he rushed towards him and grabbed him by the neck. Phebe and her mother screamed hysterically and tried to pull him off of Luke. It seemed like he had been choking him forever, but in reality, it had only been a few seconds before two nurses ran into the room to see what all of the commotion was about.

"What's going on in here?" one of them asked when she saw Phebe trying to pull Keith off of the patient.

"SECURITY!! CALL SECURITY!!" the other nurse yelled.

"Keith, please calm down before you go to jail," his mother-in-law said to no avail. About a minute or so later, two security guards ran into the room and pulled Keith off of Luke. They escorted him out of the room while the nurses tended to Luke. They walked him downstairs where they met two police officers, and he was handcuffed and placed in the back of the squad car.

One of the cops told him to sit tight until they figured out exactly what was going on. *Damn, I still didn't kill that nigga,* is what Keith kept thinking to himself while becoming angrier by the minute. He sat there for about twenty minutes before the cops came back and said anything to him. The only thing he could concentrate on was how Phebe was protecting Luke and how bad he wanted to kill them both. The door finally opened, and he heard one of the cops talking.

"It seems like you're supposed to be going to jail, but neither the patient nor the hospital is pressing charges, so you're free to go. You just can't go back inside of the hospital or within five hundred feet of anyone that was in that room," the cop said.

Upstairs, Phebe had to swallow her pride and tell them the reason for the outbreak. She felt like it was the least she could do, even though she was pissed off at Keith herself. Keith walked to his car with one of the cops following him, and he hopped in and left.

Chapter 26

It was four o'clock Saturday evening and all of the Millers were sitting at the kitchen table discussing the events that had taken place. Each of them had paired up and talked separately for brief periods of time, but they all agreed to meet up and discuss their upcoming plans in detail. For everything to work, all of them would have to be on the same page and finding out that Fred's death was caused by Malcolm was more than enough to pull them together, if only for the moment.

Cameron was still not happy about the idea of letting Malcolm come back home. It just didn't feel right, but for the plan to be successful, she had to. Tomorrow was the day she was set to call him and allow him to come over and talk. He had called a few times since Keith answered her phone, then the calls stopped and that frightened Cameron even more. Knowing what was in store, she thought it was best for Kingston not to be around, so Toya agreed to keep him for a week or however long it took, which is where he was now.

Charlotte had taken a leave of absence from work so she was present as well, along with Crystal. Taking the first step, Charlotte scheduled and took Crystal to a cancer specialist she had researched that was located in Tuscaloosa, and they would get results from the tests in about a week or so. Even though Cameron had told Charlotte that she should keep her baby, Charlotte was still undecided. The damage had been done, but she just wanted to put everything behind her and felt like bringing a baby into the drama would keep things at a standstill. A decision would have to be made soon, that much she knew.

"Cameron, I know this very difficult for you to do, but I think it's the best approach," Mr. Miller said.

Her mother grabbed her by the hand and squeezed tight. "All of this madness will be over soon sweetheart," her mom declared to her.

"Yeah, I know. I'm just ready to get it all over with," Cameron replied.

"All we have to do is treat him like normal and be sure he doesn't suspect anything. After about a week, I will handle the rest," Mr. Miller said. Cameron sat there and started thinking about what she had done in high school that left Brittany dead and figured it must run in the family. Dropping her head to her chest, *Man, KARMA IS A MOTHERFUCKING BITCH ain't it!* she screamed in her head, but really wanted to say it out loud. Although she had tampered with the wheels to cause the accident, her dad's plan still involved one of Malcolm's vehicles. The plan was for his accelerator to increase speed once he reached forty-five miles per hour. The brakes would be locked up, keeping him from being able to stop. Since Malcolm loved to drive fast anyway, an "accident" would be the perfect plan. If everything went according to plan, he would even have some alcohol in his system. Cameron started discreetly texting her girls while her dad was talking.

Cameron: What are y'all doing?

Toya: I'm reading while Kingston is watching a movie. We'll probably run to the store later. What you doing?

Sonya: Nothing really. Need to be cleaning, but I'm just sitting here.

Shay: I'm reading a book. What you up to?

Cameron: Sitting here listening to my dad go over his grand plan, feeling like tonight will be my last free night. This shit is crazy.

Toya: It will all work out. Something might happen to his crazy ass without y'all even having to do much.

Sonya: I know your nerves are shot.

Cameron: Hell yeah!

Shay: Where is Keith? Is he gonna keep you company tonight. Good sex should help relax you.

Toya: Shay!! What the hell we gon do with yo ass lol?

Sonya: She is sooo special.

Cameron: He got so much going on himself. I got something else to tell y'all too.

Toya: A little less dramatic this time, please.

Shay: Oh lord!

Sonya: What now?

Cameron: Mrs. Edwards said she did a home DNA test on Kingston....and he's Keith's son

Shay: Whaaattttt????

Sonya: Cam...say what now?

Toya: LOL!! I asked yo ass how many times was Kingston Keith's son?

Cameron: Shit, I answered too. I'm gonna have to do another test. I figured when Malcolm did the test, it was really confirmed. I didn't have any more doubts.

Toya: Malcolm ass rigged those results. His twisted ass mind. Don't get me started.

Shay: What did Keith say?

Sonya: I was just about to ask that.

Cameron: Apparently, he doesn't know yet. My dad fussing at me...I'll text y'all back when I leave here and go home. Toya I'll probably come by later on. I gotta go to the house first tho.

Toya: OK

****

While sitting in his office, Detective Young received a package with no return address. He was not in the best of moods because his informant had gone missing. He wanted to kick his own ass because he failed to hook the wire she had on up to the monitor. It was the first careless mistake that he had made on this case. It had been two days since he last heard from her. Francis had disappeared one time before for two days, so he was hoping she would show up for their meeting that was scheduled for that night. He would often have private meetings with her and have his way. He looked at it as a way to keep her in line and also sample some black pussy. Being only five feet four inches tall with a belly that looked like he was ten months pregnant didn't allow him the opportunity to freely choose women. His receding hair line didn't help matters either so whenever the opportunity presented itself, he dived into pussy that he knew he would never get on a regular day.

"What you got there?" his partner asked.

"I have no idea, and there's no return label or anything," he replied.

"Well, open it up and see," his partner said, being nosey. He knew that his partner hardly ever received anything because no one liked him, so he was curious to see exactly what he had received.

"Will you give me time?" Young replied, while opening the box.

"WHAT THE FUCK?" he frantically screamed while jumping up from his desk after opening the box.

"What is it? What's wrong?" his partner nervously asked, standing up as well and walking towards the desk. They both stared in to the box for a couple of minutes before realizing it contained the head of the informant, Francis, and her tongue had been cut out of her mouth. The letter X was drawn on her forehead.

"Those sick sons of bitches," Detective Young fumed. "I'm gonna make those bastards pay. I know Edwards is behind this shit. I just know it," he continued venting.

"I told you to wait a little while longer before sending her back out there," Young's partner said, which caused him to glare at him with rage in his eyes. "I'm just saying, you never listen. We're gonna have to talk to the captain and take a different approach now," he continued while shaking his head.

"This is some got damn bullshit," Detective Young mumbled.

Chapter 27

When Cameron left her parent's house, she called Keith as soon as she got in the car. He told her that he was going to come by later because he was in West Point at the moment. That was almost an hour away, so she told him that she was about to run in the house and get her phone charger, then go check on Kingston at Toya's house. She let him know that she had some important things to discuss with him. He told her he had some shit to tell her too. "See you later bae," she told him and disconnected the call from Bluetooth.

Pulling up at home, she turned the car off and only grabbed her house key, since she was planning on coming right back out. Walking in the house, she paused momentarily because she got an eerie feeling. *I should not be scared in my own home,* she told herself and headed down the hall to her bedroom. After grabbing her charger, she picked up her overnight bag that stays packed, just in case Keith was running too late, and she decided to stay with Toya. Opening the refrigerator to grab a Dr. Pepper, she dropped it when she turned around and locked eyes with Malcolm as he asked, "Going somewhere?"

"What... what the fuck are you doing here... here... here?" Cameron asked, trying not to show fear, but it was a losing battle because she was stuttering.

"It's my house too," Malcolm said a little too calmly. "So, you just feel like you can move on and live without me? I told you that shit wasn't going to happen," he continued. Cameron knew right then that she had to make a run for it, if she wanted to live. Bending down and picking up the soda she dropped caused him to close in on her. She picked it up and threw it at his head, hitting him in the forehead, and took off running. It only distracted him momentarily. He chased her and grabbed her by her right arm just as she was trying to get out of the front door.

"HELP HELLPPP!!! SOMEBODY HELP ME!!!" she screamed. Malcolm grabbed her by the hair and threw her hard on the love seat. He pulled a knife out of his pocket and told her not to move. "Don't make me cut you up into little pieces," he threatened her.

"I was about to let you come home tomorrow," Cameron said, as tears started rolling down her cheeks. She didn't want to appear weak at the time, but she couldn't help it because her life was on the line.

"Yeah right. You let another nigga answer your phone," Malcolm said with a sinister look in his eyes. Cameron saw her life slipping away right before her, but she knew she couldn't give up.

Damn, I should have called him yesterday just to speak like dad suggested, Cameron thought.

"We had something good. All I wanted was you; those other women never meant anything to me. Why couldn't you just love me like you did in the beginning? I didn't wanna have to kill you, but I told you what I would do," Malcolm said, as he was reaching into his pocket. Cameron noticed his slow movements and looked to her right at the lamp. POW! A bullet flew right by her head and piss started running down her legs. *Fuck this shit, I'm not going down without a fight,* Cameron thought as she picked up the lamp and threw it right at Malcolm's head, hitting him in the nose, and took off running for the back door.

Once she made it outside, she ran to the backyard at full speed. POW POW POW! Hearing gunshots, she started to run in a zig zag pattern to keep from being hit... POW POW POW POW! *Damn, how many bullets he got?* she was thinking to herself and glad it was getting a little dark. Forgetting about the wire fence that was in the distance, she ran straight into it, causing it to cut her neck, and she bounced backwards. She thought she heard Malcolm scream, like he had been hurt, but her focus was on getting away. Trying to get up and start back running, she felt Malcolm grab her feet and started dragging her back towards the house. "NOOOO!! NOOOO!!" she cried. "Please stop!! Don't do this!" she pleaded with her eyes closed.

After being dragged all the way back to the backyard, Cameron heard someone say, "I'm sorry, I wasn't trying to hurt you." Thinking she was going crazy, she started crying harder.

"Don't cry, I won't be here long," the man said. Cameron opened her teary eyes and noticed that the man didn't have his gun pointed at her, but it was pointed at Malcolm instead, who was lying down on the ground next to her with blood oozing from his stomach. "I'm going to make this quick, and I'm so sorry that I have to do this in front you, but it has to be done. My name is Johnny, and Malcolm paid me to kill your brother-"

"He's lying," Malcolm said and Johnny shot him in the other leg.

"As I was saying, he paid me to kill your brother, and I have been looking for him since. I found your dad's address and sent him a letter because I knew that he would go searching for Malcolm and lead me straight to him. I did something terrible that can't be taken back, and it's only fair that I make it right the best way I know how to. I've been following this son of a bitch and have been patiently waiting on my moment to get revenge on his black ass for using me and threatening to kill my mom," Johnny solemnly spit out.

Walking up to Malcolm, he told him to burn in hell and shot him twice in the head. "Tell your whole family that I'm so very sorry," Johnny said, right before placing a bullet in his own head. Cameron let out a gut wrenching scream, and her unshed tears would not stop falling. She cried and cried and when she realized someone had picked her up, she started to panic.

"It's me sweetheart, what happened?" her dad asked while looking at the dead bodies of Malcolm's and some other man. Cameron couldn't speak for crying so hard. "Let me call 911 baby," her dad said while holding and cradling her close to his chest.

Ten minutes later, the police and paramedics arrived on the bloody scene. A distraught Cameron had to relive what had just taken place before her eyes. She was so shaken up; it took about an hour to give them the full story. Keith had driven up and was walking near them without Mr. Miller or Cameron noticing. He was close enough to hear the story she was relaying to the police, and he was fuming on the inside, thinking that he should have killed Malcolm a long time ago. He finally walked up to them and made his presence known by putting his arms around Cameron, holding her tight.

About ten minutes later, the rest of Cameron's family showed up. Mrs. Miller brought the letter with her as evidence for the police to see and to confirm the story Cameron had given them.

"NOOOOOOO!! WHAT DID Y'ALL DO TO MY BABY?" Bertha showed up screaming loudly. She had called Malcom's phone and was told to come to the address they provided, in which she knew was his home address. "NOT MY BABY LORD!!! WHAT HAPPENED?" she continued yelling. The officers turned their focus to Bertha and informed her of the details of her son's murder. "Noooo... not my baby... he wouldn't do that... not my Malcolm," Bertha hysterically insisted. After revealing the letter and cashier's check to her, Bertha dropped to her knees and held her tightened chest. The paramedics attended to her and tried to get her to calm down. After catching her breath, Bertha got up, took off running to her car, and drove away from the house. Her cries could be heard until she was gone.

Getting their attention again, "Are you done with her? She's had enough of this shit!" Keith asked the officer, referring to Cameron.

"I think we have all we need from her for now," the officer replied. Keith wanted to get his bae away from all of the mess and the horrific scene she just witnessed. Picking her up and carrying her to his car, Keith buckled Cameron in the passenger's seat and kissed her on the forehead before getting in the driver's seat and pulling away. The rest of the Miller family stood in the backyard absolutely stunned at the events that occurred and recognized that their nightmare had finally ended.

Malcolm had met his demise without them having to put their plan in action.

"Well, JUSTICE has been served, and it couldn't have happened to a better person," Mr. Miller said quietly.

EPILOGUE

One Year Later

Balancing a new baby and returning back to school, along with being in a new place, had been difficult, but Cameron was managing it quite well. It was a blessing not to have to work a nine to five at the moment, but once she finished up with school, she would be ready to hit the work force. Her dream of becoming a lawyer had changed; she was now taking up criminal justice and she was absolutely loved the classes. Sitting in the backyard under the gazebo, Cameron was watching Kingston play with his baby sister, Kendra, in their little play area.

"You need anything baby?" Keith asked when he walked out.

"Just need you to come give me a hug and a kiss," she replied sweetly.

"You ain't said nothing but a word," he replied, as he came and granted her wishes.

After all of the madness had died down and Keith's divorce was finalized, he asked Cameron to marry him and move to Texas with him. She was hesitant at first, not wanting to rush anything, but when he found out that she was pregnant, he wasn't taking no for an answer. Another DNA test was administered to prove Kingston's paternity after all of the confusion that had taken place. Much to the Miller's and Edward's delight, the new results undoubtedly concluded that Kingston was Keith's son, and he was beyond elated. They quickly changed the birth certificate to remove Malcolm as the father and added Keith's name instead. Kingston now referred to Keith as "dad", but sometimes Unk, when he was being silly. Neither of their parents wanted them to move away, but both families understood moving was for the best, promising to visit every chance they got.

Tyler, Texas had been a nice area for them to reside in, and it was looking like they might be there for a while. Cameron had been going to therapy once a week, but now she was only going once a month because of the progress she made. Cameron cashed in her half a million-dollar life insurance policy, and Keith had almost two million dollars saved, so they were able to live comfortably. Bertha was never Cameron's favorite person, but she sent her a check for fifty thousand dollars, just because. To sever all ties with Malcolm's family, Cameron included a copy of the paternity test proving Keith was the father to prevent them from having contact with Kingston.

Keith turned in his street card and looked for better ways to provide for his family. He invested in several businesses and even invested in the stock market. He felt like his life was now complete. Living his life looking over his shoulder and being worried about who might be out to get him had gotten old. Marco was now the man in charge and word had it that he was a force to be reckoned with. Keith couldn't help but to think about Luke, knowing that position was supposed to be his. Phebe signed the divorce papers with no problem and moved to Miami with Luke. Word got around that they had a baby boy and Luke was trying to take over the street there, not realizing he was in unfamiliar territory.

Charlotte decided to move back to Mississippi to be closer to everyone. While taking her mother to one of her appointments, she met a guy who was there caring for his mom. He approached her and they began talking. Charlotte was brutally honest with him, hoping that it would run him off, but it only made him like her more. He told her that everyone has a past and he was in awe that she was so honest right away, giving him the opportunity to make the decision on his own without being deceived. When she went into labor and gave birth to a bouncing baby girl, he was right there with her like the child was his. She let him name the baby, and he chose the name Miracle. He told her that a childhood accident prevented him from having children and that's what ended his marriage of five years. Charlotte and Cameron set aside time to call each other at least once a week, and they promised to meet up as often as possible, so their children would know each other. They both admitted to their faults, forgave each other, and did everything possible to try and move forward.

Crystal's report about her cancer spreading had been mixed up with someone else's. Although her cancer had returned, treatments were needed and successful. She was now done with treatments and enjoying spending time with her grandbaby. She had an apartment about ten minutes away from Charlotte. She and Carla set aside one day a month to have lunch and things were going quite well with them. She felt like being surrounded by love helped her health tremendously.

Mrs. Miller stayed true to her word and had not contacted Stanley anymore. She agreed to attend counseling again with her husband, and they were now back on track. They renewed their vows one month ago and made a promise to communicate better with each other. Mr. Miller held up to his earlier statement he made to himself when acknowledging if Carla ever cheated on him, he would have to deal with it. However, he made it very clear that she had cashed in her cheat receipt, and it was a one-time deal. His past transgressions would not be used against him anymore and neither will hers going forward. He had grown fond of both of his daughters' significant others, but he made it a task to check on them often to make sure they were okay.

Stanley finally agreed to attend counseling sessions as well with his wife, and things actually turned around for him. When his wife finally verbally admitted to her manipulative ways and apologized, he was able to forgive her. It would be a lie to say he didn't miss Carla, but he was holding strong to his word and trying his best to do right. He admitted to his affair because he knew lying would only make things worse. Just as he suspected, his wife already knew the truth and was able to handle everything much better than he expected. As difficult as it was, the Millers and Edwards found a way to be cordial and friendly towards each other, if only for the sake of their grandchildren.

****

At the Miller's and Edward's Thanksgiving feast…

"Dear Lord,

As we gather together around this table laden with your plentiful gifts to us, we thank you for always providing what we really need and for sometimes granting wishes for things we don't really need. Today, let us especially be thankful for each other, for family and friends who enrich our lives in wonderful ways, even when they present us with challenges. Let us join together now in peaceful, loving fellowship to celebrate your love for us and our love for each other. Amen," Mr. Miller said and looked around at everyone present for thanksgiving dinner.

"Amen!" everyone said in unison.

Enjoy My Sneak Peek To My Next Series:

I'll Never Love A Dope Boy Again

Prelude

Marquez stormed into the house pissed the fuck off. "These muthafuckas think shit just supposed to fall into their laps without working for it. Taking shit that don't belong to them like I'm some soft nigga. If shit was that got damn easy, everybody would be on top," he said while throwing his glock on the dresser.

He's so fine and looks even better when he's mad, Kamora thought. Marquez stood about six feet, three inches tall and weighed in at a solid 230 pounds. All muscle. His skin was as smooth as silk and it was accented by his champagne complexion that was full of tattoos. Clearly, this man took pride in taking care of himself with his perfectly lined beard and goatee. And those eyes! Those eyes could get him anything he wanted from any woman on earth. Staring into his eyes would be equivalent to staring at two emerald gemstones. Damn, he was sexy as fuck! When you really think about it, sexy was an understatement!

"What happened baby?" his wife, Kamora, asked sweetly while walking up to him and giving him a kiss on the cheek. Kamora stood five feet, six inches tall and when she walked into a room, all eyes were immediately drawn to her. Her dazzling smile revealed the glow of her perfectly bronzed cheeks. Her medium brown complexion was absolutely flawless. Her plump luscious lips were always glossed to perfection and those chestnut eyes drove men crazy and made women envious of her. She was the type of beautiful that was hard to look away from. Not to mention, her long, jet black hair that flowed freely down her back with a few curls resting carefully over her right shoulder. Pulling him to the bed so that she could give him a massage, she told him to tell her exactly what happened. He tried not to put her in all of the street business, but she always had a way of getting the information out of him. Stressed to the max, he opened up to her without much prompting at all this time.

"This lil punk ass nigga from New Orleans decided to try and run game today. I had to bust that nigga in broad daylight. I ain't no fuck nigga and ain't no way I'm gon let some lil nigga get away with that kinda shit, and you know it. Word started spreading like wildfire after I popped his ass; now, his niggas wanna grow some balls and try to plot to take me out," Marquez fumed. "The thing is, it was Julio's lil muthafuckin brother and we squashed our beef last fuckin' year. Now, the bullshit has resurfaced, but I ain't no punk so it is what it is, ya know," he continued while shaking his head.

Kamora stood there admiring and thinking about their life while giving him a massage and listening to him vent about his street life. This was normal, and it was worse when they lived in the dead center of The Bluff. It took a lot of convincing to leave the hood, but they finally bought a four bedroom, three and a half bath, two story Victorian Style home in the Brookhaven Historic District in Atlanta. The first floor included formal living and dining areas, dramatic two story soaring ceilings, a spacious kitchen with an island and high end granite countertops throughout, the master bedroom, D'Mani's room, and a game room. Once you walk up the grand spiral staircase, you'd find two guest bedrooms, two bathrooms, a panic room, and an office. The spacious garage housed their Mercedes AMG G65 SUV's, popularly known as the G-Wagon, his black and hers white. Their other three vehicles were outside in sight. It always seemed like someone was home, even if they weren't. Kamora wondered if all of it was worth Marquez being in the street every day.

"Babe, let's go out... we can get out of the city and just relax. You need some down time and I can use some too," Kamora said after breaking herself from her thoughts.

"I would love too, but I better lay low for a few days boo," Marquez said while turning around and biting on her neck. "Where's D'Mani?" he continued.

"He's in his room sleeping," Kamora replied through her moans. "Let's go tomorrow night then; we can go to Alpharetta, Norcross, Roswell or somewhere. They're all about forty-five minutes to an hour away from the city." Kamora kept trying to get him to say yes. Wiggling from under him, she reached down and started massaging his thick dick. "Say yes," she prompted, while pulling it out and licking her lip. She bent down and licked the tip, teasing him. "Say yes," she said.

"Hell yeah! Oh shit!" he said as soon as she deep throated him. Kamora licked and sucked and swirled her tongue all over Marquez's dick until he raised up and threw her on the bed. "My turn," he said while opening up her robe to see that she was completely naked underneath. He didn't think his dick could get any harder, but it did. Tracing kisses down her firm and tight body, he momentarily stopped and asked, "Is it time to start back working on our lil princess yet?"

Kamora instantly got a little sad because she had a miscarriage a couple of months back and her doctor advised her to have two full cycles before trying again and prescribed her some Orthro Tri-Cyclen. "Next month," she finally whispered.

Noticing the immediate change in his wife's mood, Marquez turned his foreplay up a couple of notches. He inserted two fingers into her tight, wet pussy before sucking on her clit while pinching her left nipple with his free hand. "Mmmmm... oh shit!" Kamora moaned. Marquez simultaneously sucked and licked her pussy while finger fucking her until she came all in his mouth. When he was satisfied, he raised up and dove deep into the pussy. Slow, then fast, and slow again... he beat her pussy up.

"Whose pussy is this?" he asked.

"This your pussy daddy...umm," she moaned while throwing it back at him. "Let me... get on... top," Kamora moaned between his strokes. He pulled her up and let her ride without ever pulling out.

"That's it baby, get all this dick," Marquez said. She bounced up and down on his hard dick, taking in every inch of him.

"Ahhhh!" she screamed when another orgasm took over her body. He knew he was getting the best of her, so he flipped her over so he could pound her from the back.

Smacking her on the ass before entering her wetness, he said, "You better take this dick!"

"Give it to me then," she countered. And that's exactly what he did. Stroke after stroke after stroke. "I'm bout to come baby, come with me!" Kamora screamed.

"Shit... here I come ma," he said before nutting all inside of her and collapsing on her back. "Got damn! That was just what I needed," Marquez said when he finally rolled over and removed his weight off of her.

"You know we're pretty content right. You've been going hard for almost ten years," Kamora said while rubbing all over his tattoos. He knew exactly where this conversation was going and it somewhat scared him because it seemed like something bad happened every time she got the urge to talk about him getting out of the game.

"It won't be much longer baby, I promise," Marquez said while leaning over and kissing her and squeezing her tight.

The next morning, Kamora woke up to the smell of breakfast. Rolling out of bed, she went in the bathroom and washed her face, brushed her teeth, and then found her robe at the foot of the bed on the floor and smiled at memories from the night and morning before. She rolled over through the night and allowed her mouth to wake up that dick of Marquez's that she loved so much and went for round two.

"Hey mommy!" squealed D'Mani as soon as Kamora walked into the living room.

"Hey, my handsome baby." She smiled warmly at her stepson and picked him up and hugged him when he was in arms reach. That little guy melted her heart. Although she didn't give birth to him, you couldn't tell her that he didn't belong to her. He was all that she knew because his mother disappeared six months after having him and dropped him off on Marquez's doorstep with a note. Kamora had only been dating Marquez for about three months, but she took on the motherly role right away after seeing that Marquez was going to accept responsibility for the child. He claimed to have only slept with D'Mani's mom one time in exchange for a few rocks. That was four years ago; they got married two years later, and they now had the perfect family. Marquez wanted a little girl to complete the picture, and Kamora wanted to fulfill his wishes.

Walking into the kitchen, she gave her husband a kiss and took a look at what he was preparing. It was her favorite meal; French toast, eggs, and sausage. "You taking the day off?" Kamora asked after they were sitting at the dining room table eating.

"It's Saturday babe, come on now," Marquez replied.

"What time are you coming home? You promised to go out tonight, remember?" Kamora said.

"Of course I remember. I'll be home by eight. You asking Brooklyn to watch D'Mani?" he asked.

"Yeah, I'm gonna call her in a few," she responded.

Later that evening after she dropped D'Mani off with Brooklyn, Kamora was browsing through her spacious walk-in closet for the perfect outfit for the night. Her hair had been laid yesterday evening when she got off of work, and her mani and pedi were taken care of on lunch the day before. After pulling out over fifty dresses, she finally decided on a black Herve Leger sleeveless origami dress and a new pair of black Christian Louboutin pumps. Pulling out one of her jewelry boxes, she decided on the set that Marquez had bought her as an anniversary gift last month. Knowing her husband's style all too well, she laid out one of his black Brook's Brother's suits and loafers. *My baby looks even better when he puts on a suit,* Kamora smiled and thought to herself before proceeding to the bathroom.

She turned on the shower, then wrapped her hair before stepping in. The jet stream she had it set on felt like heaven against her skin. Closing her eyes, she enjoyed the feeling of the hot water. Lost in her thoughts, she didn't hear Marquez walk in the bathroom or get in the shower with her until he wrapped his arms around her. "Shit!" she said, startled.

"What you in here thinking about that you didn't notice me come in?" he asked.

"I was thinking about you," Kamora replied while turning around and kissing him sweetly, then grabbing his dick. It sprang to attention with just a simple touch from her. After cupping her breasts and squeezing tightly, Marquez pulled them together and put both of them in his mouth, sucking and biting gently at first, then a little rough. She loved that shit. "Yaahhhsss!" she screamed, not holding back because D'Mani was with Brooklyn and they were home alone. When he finished devouring her breasts, he picked her up and slid her onto his dick. She wrapped her legs around him tightly and dug her fingernails into his back while squeezing her pelvic muscles tight.

"Shit," he said, stumbling a little. Kamora laughed a little and pointed to the bench that was in the shower.

Sitting down, Kamora kept riding his dick like a stallion. "Oh my gawd... ummm," she moaned. "I'm bout to come baby! Kamora said, almost out of breath. When he knew she was satisfied, he released his nut right after her. Putting her head down on his chest, she kissed on the tattoo of her name that was on his chest, right on his heart. "I love you, baby!" she said.

"I know you do," he chuckled. "I love you too... now let's get up before I change my mind about going anywhere."

They made it to Roswell about thirty-five minutes after ten and went to this place called Taboo 2 that had great reviews online. According to the past customers, it was a lowkey chill type place where people could sing, dance, drink, and enjoy great music, all at the same time. The reviews proved to be accurate because they loved the atmosphere upon entering the establishment. After requesting a booth in the back, they let the waitress lead the way. Kamora noticed her blushing at Marquez, but she paid her no mind because she was use to women flirting with him. He was just too damn fine for his own good and his demeanor showed that he knew it too. Always respecting his wife, he smiled at the waitress to be cordial, but kept it moving.

To say the food and drinks were great would be an understatement. Kamora and Marquez started feeling themselves after eating and having a few drinks. When the DJ started playing Spend My Life With You by Eric Benet and Tamia, they both got up and started singing to each other because it was their wedding song.

"I never knew such a day could come

And I never knew such a love

Could be inside of one

And I never knew what my life was for

But now that you're here I know for sure," Marquez sang like he did at his reception.

"I never knew til I looked into your eyes

I was incomplete til the day you walked into my life

And I never knew that my heart could feel

So precious and pure

One love so real!" Kamora sang back while gazing into those beautiful eyes of his.

"Can I just see you every morning when I open my eyes

Can I just feel your heart beating beside me... every night

Can we just feel this way together till the end of all time

Can I just spend my life with you..."

"We haven't had a free night like this in forever. I'm so glad I listened to my baby and took some time to relax,"

Marquez said while hugging Kamora as they were walking down the street.

"I have so much fun and I'm glad we got out. You're always so busy in the streets; we never get a chance to have fun anymore," she said while pouting a little.

"It won't be much longer baby, I promise!" Marquez said while stopping to kiss Kamora. Neither of them saw the black Chevy Impala SS coming to a stop with its windows slowly rolling down until it was too late. Bullets started flying and people started screaming and running. Marquez shielded Kamora with his body while taking bullet after bullet to his back, then neck.

"NOOOOO!!!" Kamora screamed after seeing blood pouring from her husband's body. "OH MY GOD NOOOO!!! HELLLPPP SOMEBODY HELLPPP PLEASE!!" she cried hysterically! Marquez's body had fallen down onto hers and when she looked left, she noticed the black car just began to pull off. Getting a glimpse of the eyes of the person behind the steering wheel, a chill ran over her body. She had never seen those eyes before, but she would never forget them.

By the time the paramedics made it to scene, Kamora knew that Marquez was already gone, but her heart wouldn't accept it. "DO SOMETHING!! SAVE HIM GOT DAMMIT!!" she screamed through tears, sobbing uncontrollably. Just to try to calm her down, the paramedics attempted to perform CPR to his already lifeless body. When they covered his body up, Kamora let out a gut wrenching scream and no one could comfort her. Bystanders looked on with pity, some trying to offer words of comfort. She stood there in a daze.

"Ma'am, is there anyone you can call?" an officer asked, finally gaining her attention a little. When he put his arm around her, she started crying again. In the distance, Kamora heard other officers questioning people and asking questions like, "Did you see what type of vehicles it was?" "Do you think the young man was a target or was he an innocent bystander?" Her heart was literally torn to pieces. Although she couldn't prove it at the moment, she knew Marquez's death was a result from the incident that happened the day before and the only thing she could think was... *I'll Never Love A Dope Boy Again!!!!*

TO MY AWESOME READERS….

My first series is officially complete. I can't thank you all enough for taking a chance on me. I truly hope that you enjoyed this series as much as I enjoyed writing it. I was literally on the edge of my seat at times. It was beyond therapeutic and fun. This series will always be special to me because it was dedicated to my baby brother, and it was my very first one. Many people reached out to me saying that it seemed like I was telling their life story. The feedback has been phenomenal. I'm no love expert, but I will say, know your worth and don't settle for anything less than you know you deserve. Life will always throw curve balls, but remember to live, love, laugh, and forgive. Be happy for YOU first, and everything else will fall into place. I hope and pray that you all will stick with me as I continue my journey. I have a hot new series in the works now and I think you all are going to love it. I will release the title soon. Don't be surprised to see characters from this series in future books! ☺

As always, I want your honest feedback. Getting feedback will only help me to grow. Please leave me a review on Amazon and/ or any of my social media sites and I promise I will read them all. You may also reach me via email at authortwylat@gmail.com My Facebook, Instagram, and Twitter handles are @authortwylat

I also have a reading group on Facebook. If you would like to be added, search for Twyla T's Reading Group and send a request. We are there to have discussions, play games, interact with each other, and you can even win prizes from time to time. My new series title will be released soon.

Just in case you missed it….

Other books written by Author Twyla T

We Both Can't Be Bae

We Both Can't Be Bae 2

****

New Series Coming Soon!!! ☺

CPSIA information can be obtained
at www.ICGtesting.com
Printed in the USA
LVOW10s1759010518
575557LV00011B/720/P

9 781532 742507